I'VE WANTED YOU FOR SO LONG, MY BEAUTIFUL CECELIA . . ."

Cecelia had been kissed before—but this time the kissing was being done by an expert. She swayed against him and her arms went up to circle his neck. When the pressure of his mouth increased on hers, she parted her lips for him. His arms tightened to hold her close and she could feel the length of his lean hard body pressed against hers. He pushed the strap of her sundress aside and his hand slid down to her breast, moving caressingly, setting fire to her insides. In that moment she knew that whatever he wanted from her he could have. . .

P9-DEQ-613

JOAN WOLF is a native of New York City who presenstly resides in Milford, Connecticut, with her husband and two children. She taught high school English in New York for nine years and took up writing when she retired to rear a family.

Dear Reader:

The editors of Rapture Romance have only one thing to say—thank you! At a time when there are so many books to choose from, you have welcomed ours with open arms, trying new authors, coming back again and again, and writing us of your enthusiasm. Frankly, we're thrilled!

In fact, the response has been so great that we now feel confident that you are ready for more stories which explore all the possibilities that exist when today's men and women fall in love. We are proud to announce that we will now be publishing four titles each month, because you've told us that two Rapture Romances simply aren't enough. Of course, we won't substitute quantity for quality! We will continue to select only the finest of sensual love stories, stories in which the passionate physical expression of love is the glorious culmination of the entire experience of falling in love.

And please keep writing to us! We love to hear from our readers, and we take your comments and opinions seriously. If you have a few minutes, we would appreciate your filling out the questionnaire at the back of this book, or feel free to write us at the address below. Some of our readers have asked how they can write to their favorite authors, and we applaud their thoughtfulness. Writers need to hear from their fans, and while we cannot give out addresses, we are more than happy to forward any mail.

Happy reading!

Robin Grunder
Rapture Romance
New American Library
1633 Broadway
New York, NY 10019

CHANGE OF HEART

by

Joan Wolf

RAPTURE ROMANCE

NEW AMERICAN LIBRARY

TIMES MIRROR

PUBLISHER'S NOTE

This novel is a work of fiction. Names, characters, places, and incidents are either the product of the author's imagination or are used fictitiously, and any resemblance to actual persons, living or dead, events, or locales is entirely coincidental.

NAL BOOKS ARE AVAILABLE AT QUANTITY DISCOUNTS
WHEN USED TO PROMOTE PRODUCTS OR SERVICES.
FOR INFORMATION PLEASE WRITE TO PREMIUM MARKETING DIVISION,
THE NEW AMERICAN LIBRARY, INC., 1633 BROADWAY,
NEW YORK, NEW YORK 10019.

Copyright © 1983 by Joan Wolf

All rights reserved

SIGNET, SIGNET CLASSICS, MENTOR, PLUME, MERIDIAN and NAL BOOKS are published by The New American Library, Inc., 1633 Broadway, New York, New York 10019

First Printing, August, 1983

1 2 3 4 5 6 7 8 9

PRINTED IN THE UNITED STATES OF AMERICA

Chapter One

It was a gray, cold February afternoon and Cecelia Vargas was teaching her Wednesday after-school class of beginners when she glanced over and saw a little girl in the doorway of the riding arena. "I'll be right with you," she called. The child, and the gray-haired man accompanying her, nodded in acknowledgment.

When she had the children walking out their ponies Cecelia crossed the arena to the doorway. "Jennifer?" she asked with a smile.

"Yes," came the soft reply. Jennifer Archer was a very pretty, fair-haired nine-year-old whose deep blue eyes looked gravely back at the slim dark girl who was addressing her.

"Hi," she said. "I'm Cecelia. My father asked me to give you your lesson."

"I thought Señor Vargas was going to teach Jennifer," said the man.

Cecelia's large dark eyes moved from the child to his weather-beaten face. "Daddy never teaches the beginners," she said simply. "I'm sorry he didn't explain that to you when you called, Mr. Archer."

The ruddy face broke into a grin. "I'm not Mr. Archer, Miss Vargas. I'm the chauffeur. Name's Frank Ross. I hope you don't mind if I watch?"

"Of course not. And you needn't worry, Mr. Ross. I've been teaching children for years."

He cocked an eyebrow at her. "Can't have been for too many years, miss. But if your father says it's all right, I'll go along with it. Mr. Archer had him checked out before he allowed Jennifer to come."

Cecelia's beautiful mouth looked suddenly sardonic. Her large luminous eyes glinted. "Yes, Daddy has a good reputation," was all she said though.

Frank knew he was staring, and with an effort he turned his eyes to the little girl. "Are you ready, Jennifer?" he asked.

"Yes," the child said again.

Cecelia looked at her quiet little face and smiled warmly. Frank felt himself staring once again. "Come along with me, Jenny, and we'll find you a hat," Cecelia said. "If you're going to continue riding you'll have to get one. I have very strict rules about riding with a hat." They moved off together across the stable yard.

The lesson was successful and Jennifer made an appointment to ride again the following afternoon. Cecelia told her father about it as they sat together over dinner that evening. "She's a very quiet child," she added, "but she seemed to like it."

"If she's coming again tomorrow she must have liked it," her father responded.

"Gilbert Archer had you checked out before he

allowed her to come." She cocked an amused eyebrow at him. "The chauffeur expected you to handle the lesson."

"Oh?" Ricardo raised his eyebrows in an identical gesture. They were still black even though his thick hair had long since begun to gray. "Did you explain that you taught all the beginners?" His English was fluent, with only the slightest hint of an accent to betray his Argentine origins.

"Yes. And he graciously allowed me to do the job. Gilbert Archer would probably have insisted on you."

Ricardo finished the last of the stew on his plate. "Men like Gilbert Archer are accustomed to commanding only the best." He put his knife and fork down and smiled at his daughter. "And in you that is what he has gotten, *niña*."

She smiled back affectionately. "Do you want some more stew, Daddy?"

"Please."

She took his plate and went over to the stove. "Poor little Jennifer," she said. "I feel sorry for her. She seems such a perfect example of the 'poor little rich girl' syndrome."

"What makes you say that?" Ricardo asked.

"Marie Rice, Major's owner, teaches at Central Grammar and she has Jennifer in class. She says the child is painfully quiet. It can't have been easy on her, losing her mother in a car crash and then being sent to live with a father she hardly knew."

"It must be difficult for a man as busy as Gilbert Archer to find time for a child," Ricardo agreed. "But that doesn't mean he doesn't care for her. He moved to Connecticut so that she would be out of New York and in the country. Surely that says something. I'm sure the commute into the city is a nuisance for him."

"How do you know why he moved?" Cecelia asked curiously.

"Jim Johnson at Berkeley Realtors sold him The Birches." Jim Johnson had been a friend of Ricardo's for years. "He paid a small fortune for it, I might add."

"I imagine he must have," Cecelia agreed. "But I wonder how much time *he* spends there."

"He is a busy and important man," Ricardo said calmly. "Such men, in my experience, are rarely home."

Cecelia rose to clear away the dishes. "Poor Jennifer," she repeated as she stacked them in the sink. She had lost her own mother when she was ten, which was one of the reasons she felt such sympathy for Jennifer. She smiled at her father and said, "I always had you."

He smiled back. "What's for dessert?" he asked.

"Ice cream," she replied and opened the refrigerator.

Conversation in the kitchen of The Birches was revolving around the riding lesson as well. "How did Jennifer do this afternoon?" Nora Ross asked her husband. The Rosses had been with Gilbert Archer for the last five years, ever since Frank had retired from the army. Nora functioned as housekeeper and cook and Frank as chauffeur and handyman. Since the death of the ex-Mrs. Archer eight months ago, the Rosses' chores had come to include looking after Jennifer as well.

"Very well," Frank replied. "Vargas didn't give her the lesson, his daughter did. But she seemed to know what she was doing. Jennifer talked about it all the way home."

"Did she?" Nora was surprised; like Cecelia, the Rosses too had found Jennifer to be unusually quiet.

"Yes. She made an appointment to go tomorrow as well. I'll check it out with Mr. Archer, but I don't think he'll mind."

"He'll be glad she's found something she likes to do," Nora prophesied.

Frank grinned teasingly at his wife. "I'll tell you what, Nora. I won't mind if Jennifer wants to take a lesson every day."

Nora peered at him closely. "Why?"

"Cecelia Vargas," he answered simply, "is the most beautiful girl I've ever laid eyes on in my life."

"You old goat," his wife said with amused affection. "Eat your dinner."

When Gilbert Archer came home that evening it was after nine-thirty, but he went anyway to peek into his daughter's room. She was still awake. "Hi, Daddy," she said from her pretty white-painted bed.

"You should be asleep, sweetheart," he answered, but he came into the room and sat on the edge of the bed.

"I had a riding lesson today, Daddy," the little girl said. "It was super."

"Was it?" He looked thoughtfully at her suddenly vivacious face.

"Yes. I'm going tomorrow, too. Cecelia says I need a hat, though. And boots. Can I get them, Daddy?"

"Sure," he answered. "Who is Cecelia?"

"She's the girl who's teaching me. She's super too."

"I thought Señor Vargas was going to give you your lesson," her father said, his fair brows slightly knitted.

"Cecelia says he never teaches beginners. She's his daughter, you know. Frank said she knows her stuff."

Gilbert Archer could not ever remember seeing his daughter this animated. "Well, I'm glad you liked it, Jen. I'll tell Nora to take you shopping for the proper clothes." He bent his head to kiss her, and for a moment the two silver-blond heads were close together on the pillow. "Good night, sweetheart," he murmured softly.

"Good night, Daddy."

Two months later Cecelia was working a big chestnut gelding over some jumps in the arena when a woman appeared in the doorway. She watched with undisguised interest as Cecelia took the horse over a spread fence, then circled him and made him take it again, this time taking off much closer to the jump. "Good boy!" she said, patting him approvingly. She began to walk him out and the woman led her own horse into the arena and swung up into the saddle. "Czar is looking good," she called to Cecelia as she began to walk her gray around the ring.

"Isn't he?" Cecelia called back. "If I can only get him to wait on the spreads!"

Marie Rice eased her horse in next to Cecelia's. "I've been meaning to tell you what a good job you're doing with Jennifer Archer. She's even started to lose some of her shyness in school."

Cecelia smiled. "I'm glad to hear that. She's a darling child."

"She's a very lonely child," said Marie.

"It's hard, at that age, to lose your mother." Cecelia's lovely face was somber.

"From what I hear, Jennifer's mother was no loss," replied Marie bluntly. "She and Gilbert Archer were divorced when Jennifer was two and she went on to play around with a whole series of other men. She was the type who spent the winter skiing at St. Moritz, the spring shopping in Paris, and the summer cruising on somebody's private yacht."

"But where was Jennifer?" asked Cecelia in a startled voice.

"Home with the servants."

"Oh." Cecelia leaned forward to feel if Czar was still hot. "From what I gather, the situation hasn't changed much. The chauffeur brings her here and takes her home."

"Yes. Well to be fair, Gilbert Archer is a busy man. And at least he's spending his time doing something worthwhile, not just jet-setting around the world."

"I suppose that's true. *News Report* is a very highly regarded magazine. Daddy says it's the only North American journal that has even an inkling of what Latin America is all about."

"I've been taking it for years," Marie answered. "Well, come on, Major, time for your morning exercise. I have to be at school in an hour and a half." She urged the gray into a trot while Cecelia dismounted and led Czar back to the barn.

As she curried his coat she reflected on some of the things Marie had told her. She knew that Jennifer's parents had been divorced and, unconsciously, she had assumed the fault was Gilbert Archer's. She had done some reading up on him since Jennifer had begun to ride at Hilltop Farm and had discovered that the founder and editor of *News Report* was a very powerful and influential man indeed. His magazine was one of the most widely respected journals in the country, famous for its in-depth and balanced reporting, and its editor was known for personally reporting on many stories himself. Cecelia had seen his picture on several occasions now, and had been surprised by his youth. She had supposed he must be an older man, but according to the article she had read recently in the *Times* he was only thirty-five.

She finished doing Czar and put him in his stall with his blanket on. She patted his nose, murmured, "You can go out and play later," and left the barn, carefully closing the door to keep the heat in. She wondered briefly if Gilbert Archer ever planned to come by and see how his daughter was progressing.

He came that afternoon. Jennifer had joined the five other girls in Cecelia's beginners class, and the ponies were all trotting briskly around the ring when a tall, leanly built man appeared in the arena doorway. "Half seat everyone," Cecelia called, and as the children all leaned forward into jumping position she noticed the stranger. She was just about to ask if she could help him when Jennifer called, "Hi, Daddy!"

"Hi, sweetheart," he returned in a deep and pleasant voice.

So this was Gilbert Archer. Cecelia stared curiously at him from her position in the middle of the arena. He wore a tan golf jacket over brown corduroy pants. His hands were in his pockets and he looked very much at ease as he stood there in the wide doorway, his eyes on his daughter. Cecelia's eyes followed his. "Flatten your back, Jenny," she called. Then: "That's right. That looks good." Her eyes went to the next child. "Stand in your heels, Meredith, not your irons," she commanded and the lesson continued.

At five-thirty Cecelia called a halt and Jenny walked her pony over to her father. They exchanged a few words and then the little girl began to walk the pony out. Gilbert Archer remained in the doorway.

"Make sure they all have their blankets on," Cecelia instructed the children, "and be sure the tack is cleaned properly. Meredith, Sunday gets his feet oiled." She picked up her appointment book and began to walk purposefully toward the man in the doorway. "Hello, Mr. Archer," she said as she reached him. "I'm Cecelia Vargas." She held out her hand.

He looked like his pictures, but what the pictures didn't show was the indefinable aura of easy authority and power that he exuded. His thin, chiseled face was surprisingly suntanned, his chin had a cleft in it that she had not noticed in his photographs, and his eyes were not blue like Jennifer's but a light gray.

She looked at him with the unself-conscious gaze of a child, completely unaware of the picture she herself presented in her red sweater with her hair pulled loosely off her face and falling in a long braid down her back.

"So you are 'Cecelia says'! . . ." His voice had a thread of amusement in it. He took her hand in his; it was warm from his pocket and his clasp was firm.

"I beg your pardon?" she said, puzzled.

"Every other word out of Jennifer's mouth lately has been 'Cecelia says,'" he explained with deepening amusement. "I have been quite anxious to meet you."

Cecelia smiled. "Oh dear, I certainly didn't mean to be a disruptive influence."

He shook his head. "Far from it, Miss Vargas. In fact, I am grateful to you. You have been very good for Jennifer."

"I like her," Cecelia said simply.

He looked at her for a moment in silence, a small line between his brows. Then he said, rather abruptly, "I wonder if I might talk to you for a few minutes."

"Certainly," Cecelia responded courteously. "Jenny will be a half hour at least doing the tack and the pony. If you'd care to come up to the house with me, I'll make you a cup of coffee."

"That would be very nice." He fell into step with her as she walked up the path that led to the house.

Cecelia took him in the back door, which opened directly into the kitchen. She kicked off her rubber moccasins at the door and went in stocking feet over to the stove. As she lit the gas under the kettle she said over her shoulder, "Have a seat, Mr. Archer. I'm just going to throw a log on the stove to warm the room up."

Gilbert Archer sat down at the kitchen table and watched her slim jean-clad figure bending to the iron stove that stood in the corner of the kitchen. As she came back to the table he remarked, "Ever since I've moved to Connecticut I've seen more wood-burning stoves!"

She laughed and sat down. "It's New England's only natural resource." She unsnapped her blue down vest. "I'd introduce you to my father but he's out at a meeting of the AHSA," she said, as if some explanation on the subject of her father were due.

"What is the AHSA?" he asked. She thought he had one of the most pleasant voices she had ever heard.

"The American Horse Shows Association," she answered. "Daddy is a director."

"I see." He raised an eyebrow. "It sounds like an important position."

"Well, it is rather. The AHSA is the governing body of the sport in the United States, you see."

The kettle began to whistle and she rose to make the coffee. The kitchen had begun to get warmer and Gilbert Archer took off his golf jacket and hung it over the back of the kitchen chair. Cecelia noticed with approval the color of his smoky green crew-neck sweater. She put a mug of coffee

in front of him and went to the refrigerator for
milk, then reseated herself and added both milk
and suger to her cup. He took his black, she
noticed. "Do you mind if I smoke?" he asked.

Cecelia hated to be asked that question. She did
mind but politeness forbade her saying so. "Of
course not," she said a little woodenly. "I'll find
you an ashtray."

He put the pack away. "Never mind." His gray
eyes regarded her gravely. "I have been very worried about Jennifer," he began. "She's so quiet. It
isn't natural for a little girl to be as quiet as she is."

"I know. But she's starting to come out of her
shell. She was actually giggling in the tack room
with the other kids yesterday."

"Coming here has been very good for her," he
said. She looked down at his hand, cupped now
around the coffee mug. It was a slender hand,
with beautiful long fingers, yet it looked as hard
as iron.

"She has a natural aptitude for riding," Cecelia
said, raising her eyes to his face. "Even Daddy
remarked on it the other day—and he doesn't
usually notice the beginners much. And she loves
the horses."

"It isn't just the horses she loves," returned Gilbert Archer. "As I said earlier, you have been very
good to her."

Cecelia's cheeks flushed a delicate rose. "It's been
my pleasure," she said formally.

His gray eyes were steady on her face. "She told
me you went in to see her school play this week."

"Yes, well, all the other children had mothers
who would be going," Cecelia explained. "I had

fun. The kids did a terrific job." A thought struck her. "I hope you don't object? I certainly don't want to push my way into Jenny's life if you don't like it."

There was a pause and then he gave her an absolutely charming smile. "But I do like it," he said softly. "I like it very much indeed. In fact, one of the reasons I came by today was to ask if you'd care to have dinner with Jennifer and me tomorrow evening." Cecelia hesitated, strangely affected by that smile and uneasy because of it. "Jennifer will be so disappointed if you can't make it," he added.

"I'd love to," said Cecelia.

"Wonderful. We'll pick you up at seven?"

"Fine."

He grinned, looking suddenly very young. "It will probably be that hamburger place in town— the one that has popcorn on the table. Jennifer loves it."

She smiled back. "I know it well. Daddy always took me there too. I loved the funny mirrors."

"The food isn't bad," he said ruefully. "It's the smell of the popcorn that gets to me."

She laughed. "Do they still show cartoons?"

"They do. And they've added video games as well."

"It sounds like fun," she said.

A smile fleetingly appeared in his eyes. "I should infinitely prefer Gaston's. I must be getting old," he said.

Cecelia looked back at him, the smile on her lips not matched by the gravity of her eyes. He wasn't old at all, she thought. He was in fact disconcertingly young and good-looking. She stood up. "The children should be finished with the ponies by now."

He rose as well. "I'll go and collect Jennifer then. And we'll see you tomorrow night."

"I'll be looking forward to it, Mr. Archer."

He stopped with his hand on the doorknob. "Please, won't you call me Gil? I'm afraid I can't think of you as anything but Cecelia."

She grinned mischievously. "As in 'Cecelia says' . . . I see your point . . . Gil."

He raised a hand in brief farewell, then stepped through the door and closed it firmly behind him.

Chapter Two

❧

Gil and Jennifer picked her up promptly at seven, with Gil coming to the front door while Jennifer remained in the car. Cecelia answered his ring, waved at Jennifer and said, "I'm all ready, but won't you come in for a minute and meet my father?"

"I'd like to," he replied easily and followed her into a large, high-ceilinged living room that had a roaring fire going in the huge brick fireplace. Ricardo Vargas rose from his armchair by the fire and came across the room to shake hands.

"Daddy, this is Gilbert Archer, Jennifer's father," said Cecelia. "My father, Ricardo Vargas."

"How do you do, Mr. Archer," said Ricardo gravely and looked assessingly at the other man out of eyes as dark as Cecelia's.

Gil realized with a flash of amusement that he was being sized up as to his suitability as an escort. With sudden insight he realized that all Cecelia's dates must first have to "meet Daddy." And if Ricardo Vargas didn't approve, he had a suspicion that that was the end of that particular date. "How do you do, Señor Vargas," he said. "Jennifer and I are delighted that Cecelia consented to have dinner with us this evening. She has been so good for my daughter. I am very grateful."

Ricardo Vargas's rather hard aquiline features softened. "She has a tenderness for children, Cecelia," he said. "I am glad she has helped your daughter."

"Well, we'd better get going, Daddy," Cecelia said cheerfully, not at all discomposed at being spoken about as if she were not present. "Jenny is in the car."

"Of course. You must not keep the child waiting." He took Cecelia's coat, helped her on with it, and then accompanied them to the door. "Enjoy your dinner," he said.

"Thank you, Señor Vargas," replied Gil.

"We will, Daddy," said Cecelia.

They both walked down the steps to the waiting car and Jennifer.

Cecelia did enjoy her dinner. It was fun being part of a family group, gratifying to see Jenny's blue eyes sparkle with happiness, and extremely pleasant to find herself the object of Gilbert Archer's attention. The two adults had steak; Jenny had a specialty hamburger and mountains of popcorn. Over the hamburger she conducted an inquisition of Cecelia.

"Did you go to Central Grammar too when you were a little girl, Cecelia?" she asked with unabashed curiosity.

Cecelia slowly cut herself another piece of steak. "Yes, Jenny, I did."

"Where did you go after that? My mother always said I would go away to school. Did *you* go away?"

"No. I went to Notre Dame High School in the next town. I took a bus there and back each day."

"I don't want to go away to school either," Jenny said defiantly and stared at her father. "I like living at home."

"Well, we have a few years before we have to worry about your next school," Gil said diplomatically. "We'll cross that bridge when we come to it."

"Everybody has to leave home at some point, Jenny," Cecelia said gently.

"*You* haven't," Jenny pointed out.

Cecelia laughed. "That's true. But I'm an unusual case. And I *did* spend a year in Colombia when I was in college."

"That must have been interesting," murmured Gil.

"It was. Very. It was part of an exchange program run by the Spanish Department of my college. The nuns who run Mount St. Mary's also have a college in Bogotá. I spent my junior year there."

"You were a Spanish major in college?"

"Yes. It was easy. I grew up speaking both Spanish and English—Daddy saw to that. So I was able to skip most of the language classes and concentrate on literature and history."

"Is your father from Colombia?"

"No. Argentina."

"How come he came to America?" asked Jennifer.

"He came to America when he married my mother," Cecelia explained. "Mother was on one of the first civilian United States Equestrian Teams and Daddy rode for Argentina. They met on the European circuit in 1957 and were married shortly after that."

"Your father was in the Argentine army?" asked Gil.

"Yes. He wanted to ride internationally, you see."

"Has he been back to Argentina?"

Cecelia's lovely face looked very somber. "He can't go back. Not while this government is in power."

"The army is in power. Surely if he was an army officer . . ."

"He was not a very popular army officer," Cecelia said and now she looked grim. "Nor was his family supportive of the military dictatorship. Two of my cousins were among the *desáparecidos*."

"I am very sorry," Gil said quietly.

"What are *desáparecidos*?" Jenny queried in puzzlement.

Cecelia did not answer and after a minute Gil said, "The word means 'disappeared ones.' In Argentina the people who spoke out against the government were often arrested by the army and never heard from again. They 'disappeared.' "

"You mean nobody knows where they are?"

"The government knows," Cecelia replied a little harshly. "They are probably dead. Considering what ones knows about prison conditions in Argentina, one can only pray that they are dead."

Jenny opened her mouth to ask another question, then stopped as she saw her father shaking his head at her. A little silence fell and then Gil said pleasantly, "Your father must be quite a horseman."

The grim look faded from around Cecelia's lovely mouth. "He is," she replied proudly. "He won the Grand Prix of Aachen, the King George V Challenge Cup, and the Olympic Gold Medal for Best Individual Rider in Stockholm in 1956."

"Very impressive." Gil's gray eyes were regarding her thoughtfully. "Do you have Olympic ambitions, Cecelia?"

She laughed and shook her head. "I'm not eligible. Only amateurs can qualify for the USET, and because I teach I'm regarded as a professional."

"That's too bad," he said neutrally.

"Daddy feels badly about it," she confided, "but I don't, not really. Daddy has to have help to run the barn and the school. And I *do* compete in the Open Jumper division. In fact, Daddy just bought me a gorgeous new horse. He's going to take everything in sight, I think."

Gil looked at her appraisingly for a minute as they both sipped their wine. She was wearing a burgundy turtleneck sweater that beautifully set off her rose-olive complexion. Her dark brown hair, so heavy and soft and smooth, hung down her back in a shining mantle. Small gold earrings and a ring were all the jewelry she wore.

"You look like a Renaissance madonna," he said coolly. "Has anyone ever told you that?"

She gave him a startled look. The sudden change of topic, the compliment delivered in that objective tone, disconcerted her. He sensed her confusion and moved smoothly to her assistance. "Do you do anything else besides ride horses and teach other people to ride them?"

"Well, that's all I've done since I graduated last

June," she said in a relieved tone of voice. She wanted to get the conversation off herself and added, "It must sound very dull to you. I imagine editing a magazine like *News Report* is very exciting."

"It's very hectic," he said. "When I started it eight years ago I didn't know what I was getting into."

"You must be very proud of it," she said sincerely. "In my history courses at college the professors always cited it for honest and factual reporting."

He looked pleased. "Did they? That's nice to hear."

"What made you want to publish a news magazine?" she asked curiously. She knew from her reading up on him that Gilbert Archer had been born to millions. The Archers were one of the old New York banking families and he was the only child. What had prompted such a man to ignore banking and turn his energies to a magazine like *News Report*? It had not been a decision at all popular with his father, or so she had read.

He had been asked that question often before, by women and by men, and he had a variety of answers to produce. To Cecelia he told part of the truth. She listened to him attentively, her eyes steady on his face. The wall sconce shone down on his thick hair, gilded to a gleaming silver in the soft light. There was no gray in it, she noticed. She watched his eyes, his ironic, humorous mouth, his firm chin indented by that fascinating cleft. "It seemed to me that most of our news magazines had 'sold out' to popular culture," he was saying. "At twenty-six one can be very arrogant."

"It isn't arrogant to want to do something better

than others have done it," she replied softly. "Or if it is, then it is only the arrogant who achieve excellence."

He looked thoughtfully into her eyes and was about to say something when Jennifer returned to their table. She had been playing Pac-man for the last fifteen minutes. "Guess what, Cecelia," she said as she slid in next to her, "Jessica Fox is here with her folks. She was playing Pac-man with me."

"Who is Jessica Fox?" Gil inquired.

"She's in my riding class and in my class at school," returned Jenny. Then, proudly, she added, "She's my best friend."

Cecelia smiled down at Jennifer's happy face, a smile full of amused tenderness. There was an odd expression in Gil's eyes as he watched them. Then he said to Jennifer, "Are you ready to go? It's getting late."

"I guess so." Jennifer heaved a sigh. "This was fun."

"Yes," said Cecelia, her eyes on Jennifer but her mind on Gil. "It was."

Chapter Three

She didn't see him again for two weeks. She was disappointed, and angry with herself for feeling disappointed. What would a man like Gilbert Archer see in her? What could possibly prompt him to want to seek out her company again? Their dinner together, so fascinating and important to her, had been just a casual evening to him, something done to please his daughter.

She had just decided that she would probably never see him again when he came to pick Jennifer up from her riding lesson on Friday. The sight of his tall, fair-haired figure in the doorway of the arena caused Cecelia's breath to catch for a minute in her throat. I'm behaving like an idiot, she told herself sternly. And when the lesson was over she walked toward him slowly, gathering her composure, determined to be friendly but reserved.

"Are you playing chauffeur today?" she asked with what she hoped was a casual smile.

"Yes. I got home early for once." He looked down at her gravely. She was of average height, but he made her feel small. "I've been in Washington this last week," he said.

"Oh." She bent to pick up a rock and throw it out of the arena. "I suppose you have to do a lot of traveling."

"Well, sometimes it's best to be on the scene yourself."

"Yes, I imagine so."

"Cecelia!" It was Meredith Holmes calling from the doorway of the barn. "Should I put anything on this cut of Hansi's?"

"Excuse me," Cecelia murmured to Gil and went across the stable yard to the barn. He could hear her saying something to the child and then saw her go into the barn and Meredith walk off toward the tack room. Gil slowly followed Cecelia.

The roan pony was on cross ties in the aisle and Cecelia was looking carefully at his flank. Meredith returned with a jar which Cecelia took from her. She began to apply the salve to the horse's injury. He sidled and threw up his head, but she talked soothingly to him as she worked. Finally she stepped back. "It's looking much better," she said. She caressed the pony briefly. "Make sure you put his blanket on," she told Meredith and came to stand beside Gil. "This is the pony barn," she said to him. "Would you like to see the rest of the place?"

He smiled courteously and said, "Yes."

She gave him the complete tour, including three barns and the tack room. They ended up before the stall of a big chestnut gelding. "This is Czar," she said. At the sound of her voice the gelding pricked his ears forward and came to the front of his stall. "Czar," she crooned in a soft lovely voice. The horse blew gently and she reached into her pocket for a carrot. "Piggy," she said affectionately as he chomped on it. She turned to Gil. "Czar is the new jumper I was telling you about. Isn't he marvelous?"

Gil had learned to ride one summer at camp when he was a boy, but horses had never been one of his interests. "He's beautiful," he said dutifully. Two teenage girls were deftly forking hay into the stalls and the sounds of animal munching began to fill the barn.

"Jenny must be finished by now," Cecelia said and began to walk again in the direction of the tack room.

He walked beside her, hands in the pockets of his corduroy pants. "Someone gave me a pair of tickets to *Rio*," he said, mentioning a Broadway play that was sold out for months in advance. "You said the other night that you'd like to see it. They're for tomorrow night. Would you care to go with me?"

Her brown eyes lit up. "*Rio!* I'd love to see it. But tomorrow . . ." She frowned a little. She had a date for tomorrow night.

He read her thoughts. "Cancel it," he recommended laconically.

She laughed. "I think I will. Tim won't mind. He can see me anytime."

He raised his brows at that but said nothing. Jenny came out of the tack room and called, "I'm ready, Daddy."

"I'll pick you up tomorrow at five-thirty. We can

have dinner before the show," he said to Cecelia
and walked over to where his daughter awaited
him.

Frank was driving the BMW when Gil arrived
the following evening to pick her up. Cecelia
greeted him as she got into the car. "I suppose
you're the one who's going to be stuck looking for
a parking space," she said with a smile.

"You're exactly right, Miss Vargas," he answered.
"Mr. Archer's temper can't handle New York
traffic."

Cecelia shot a look at Gil as he sat beside her.
He looked faintly amused. "Where are we going
for dinner?" she asked curiously. "I've never eaten
in a real New York restaurant."

"You haven't?" He looked surprised. "You only
live about an hour away. Surely you go into the
city sometimes."

"Of course. We go in every year for the National Horse Show at the Garden. And I've been
to some plays and the ballet. But I've never eaten
anywhere but in Howard Johnson's. Too expensive," she concluded succinctly.

"Well, we're not going to Howard Johnson's,
that I can promise you. Or to a place that serves
popcorn as an hors d'oeuvres." In the dim light of
the car she saw his finely cut nostrils quiver dis-
gustedly and she laughed. "I'm taking you to a
little French restaurant in the theater district. It's
really quite good. I hope you like French food?"

"Who doesn't?" returned Cecelia immediately.
Her eyes were luminous with pleasure.

The hour's ride into the city passed quickly.

Cecelia again found herself surprised at how easy he was to talk to. She had expected to feel shy and uncertain in his company, with no Jennifer to provide a distraction. But she felt quite comfortable, only a little keyed up and excited by the novelty of the whole expedition and the undoubted magnetism of Gilbert Archer's presence.

The French restaurant lived up to all her expectations. The maître d' recognized Gil at once. "Good evening, Mr. Archer," he said. "Your table is right this way, sir." He led them to a quiet, dimly lit table in the corner. Gil took Cecelia's cherry-colored wool reefer coat and handed it to the maître d'. As Cecelia sat down she cast a swift glance around the room to see if she were properly dressed. After a brief inspection of the other women diners she decided that her oyster-white crepe dress would do and she turned back to Gil, her soft lips parted in a small happy smile.

She was wearing her hair drawn back off her face in a smooth chignon and the style made her look older and more sophisticated than he had seen her look before. It also emphasized the largeness of her eyes and the exquisite lines of her cheekbones, jaw, and throat. "What do you usually do for fun, Cecelia, if you don't come into the city?" he asked unsmilingly.

"I stay pretty local, mostly," she replied readily enough. "Movies, neighborhood restaurants, parties at friends' houses, things like that. The horses keep me pretty busy. I don't have all that much time for outside activities."

The waiter came to take their order. "Would you like a drink?" Gil asked her.

"I'll have a daiquiri," she answered.

"A martini with a twist," said Gil. Then, as the waiter moved away, "Who is Tim?"

For a moment Cecelia looked bewildered. "Tim?"

"The guy you had a date with tonight."

Her brow cleared. "Oh, *that* Tim. He's just a friend of mine. We go out sometimes."

The waiter reappeared with their drinks and the menus. Cecelia opened hers and nearly fainted at the prices. She stared at Gil with horrified eyes and, reluctantly, he laughed. "Order what you want," he said. "I told you this wasn't a popcorn place."

"I can see that," she answered and regarded the menu dubiously once again.

"Can you read it?" he asked. It was written entirely in French.

"Oh yes. I took French in school." She glanced up at him from under her lashes, a charming, unconsciously seductive look. "It's the prices, not the language, that have me floored."

His face was inscrutable as he watched her. "I told you to forget about the prices."

"Well you asked for it," she replied cheerfully. "Damn the torpedoes and full speed ahead. I'll start with the artichoke. . . ."

They finished their coffee at ten minutes to eight. "That was sumptuous." Cecelia sighed as Gil helped her into her coat. She looked at him over her shoulder, her lips curving with pleasure.

He did not smile back. "I'm glad you enjoyed it," he said. Then, putting a hand on her arm, he began to guide her out of the restaurant. Neither of them noticed the woman seated along the wall who had been watching them closely for the last hour.

The play was as wonderful as its reviews had promised, and Cecelia sat enchanted during the entire three acts. When she accompanied Gil out into the lobby during the two intermissions so he could have a cigarette, he introduced her to several people, but their names and faces were a blur to Cecelia. She was too caught up in the play to spare much attention for strangers. She smiled politely, answered a few questions, and returned eagerly to her seat at the sound of the bell.

Frank was waiting for them outside with the BMW. "My, this is service," said Cecelia admiringly as she got into the backseat.

"Well, where to now?" Gil asked as he got in beside her. "Would you like to go to a nightclub?"

She turned great startled eyes on him. "A nightclub! But it's late already."

In the dimness of the car she could just make out his sardonic look. "It's only eleven-thirty, Cecelia."

"Yes, but we won't be home until twelve-thirty. And I have to be up tomorrow at five. I'd really rather go home, Gil, if you don't mind."

"But I do mind," he replied softly. "Don't you think it's time you let yourself live a little?"

She looked for a minute in silence at his face, so close to hers in the confines of the car. She was suddenly intensely aware of his nearness and tallness. The light from a street lamp shone in the car window, illuminating his silver-blond hair. He was, she thought abruptly, everything that a man ought to be. "I have a horse show to ride in tomorrow," she said slowly. "It's a registered show and an important one. If I want to ride Czar in the National in November he needs the points. Daddy will be angry if I'm home too late."

He leaned a little closer. "Do you always do what Daddy wants, Cecelia?"

"Yes," she answered simply. "After all, he *is* my father." She raised her beautiful winged brows at him. "You'll want Jennifer to do the same in a few years time, you know."

His face relaxed into reluctant amusement. "*Touché*," he said. "We'll go home."

They talked desultorily as the car weaved its way through the city streets. Cecelia was feeling very sleepy, and as the car moved onto the highway she gave the abrupt half sigh—half yawn of a child. A strong arm came around her. "Why don't you just go to sleep, baby?" said a deep voice in her ear. "I'll wake you when we're home."

The invitation was irresistible and she allowed her head to sink down on his shoulder. It felt so comfortable there, so natural. In three minutes she was asleep.

The society gossip column of the Monday morning New York *Daily News* ran this interesting item: "Who was the lovely brunette seen dining with Gil Archer at Chez Guillaume's last Saturday night? Gil certainly looked attentive. Are you holding out on us, darling?"

Cecelia, who did not take the paper and who would not have read the gossip column even if she had, remained in ignorance of her sudden notoriety. The item was cause for comment, however, between Liz Lewis, Gil's longtime friend and sometime mistress, and Pat Carruthers, who had been with her husband Ben at the Saturday evening performance of *Rio*.

"Did you see Betsy Bartlett's column yesterday?" Pat asked Liz as they lunched together at the Cosmopolitan Club. Both women had graduated from Radcliffe the same year Gil graduated from Harvard. Liz had made a marriage that turned out as disastrously as Gil's, and for the last few years he had been her most frequent escort. Pat knew she had hopes of becoming the second Mrs. Archer.

"Of course I did," replied Liz, regarding her cold salmon with a frown. "I didn't pay any attention to it. Gil can't sneeze without the gossip columnists making a headline out of it."

"Well this girl *was* a little out of his ordinary line," Pat said disingenuously. She genuinely liked Liz but she was also an incurable gossip.

Liz put down her fork. "Oh? Did you see her?"

"At the theater," Pat replied serenely. She chewed reflectively on her veal. "Ben told me that Gil pulled some high-powered strings to get tickets, so naturally I was curious."

"Well?" Liz demanded. "What was she like?"

"Young," replied Pat succinctly. "Very young. She can't be over twenty-three."

Liz's mouth and jaw had a tense look about them. "I didn't know Gil had a Lolita complex."

"*All* men do to some extent, don't you think? And then she is very beautiful. Ben couldn't keep his eyes off her."

Liz stared into her friend's face. "Who is she?"

"I don't know. He introduced her as Cecelia Vargas."

"Vargas?" Liz's brows snapped together. "Is she Spanish?"

"With that name, and her looks, I should say her background was most definitely Spanish. But she's American. One can always tell."

"Damn," said Liz. She ate a little of her salmon. "But then, he may only be amusing himself. Gil is hardly a Sir Galahad when it comes to women."

"That's certainly true," replied Pat. She felt a sudden pang for having enjoyed herself so much at her friend's expense. "Gil is far too sophisticated to be interested for long in a mere *jeune fille*," she comforted. "She's probably a novelty. I doubt if he'll even see her again."

Both Pat and Liz would have been extremely surprised to see the urbane and sophisticated Gilbert Archer the following Saturday. He went to a horse show. Not the socially glamorous New York National, but a local show in the hills of Connecticut which was attended primarily by little girls on ponies. He was rather surprised to be there himself.

Hilltop Farm had quite a few riders entered and Jennifer was dying to go—that was his excuse. The real reason, he admitted a little ruefully to himself as he stepped gingerly over a steaming pile in the roadway, was that he wanted to see Cecelia again.

He was a little astonished by his own behavior.

If she had been any other woman he would simply have asked her out to dinner again, but he had an uneasy feeling that if he did that she would say no. He was extremely conscious of the fact that she was twenty-two years old, thirteen years younger than he. She went out with boys whom she knew from college. And she had an extremely protective father whom he suspected would not allow her to go on seeing a man as worldly and experienced as Gil undoubtedly was.

His uncertainty about Cecelia was one experience Gil was unfamiliar with. Usually women found him all too desirable. It was that very desirability that had done in his marriage. After the first fiery sexual passion between Barbara and him had been satisfied, the trouble started. Jennifer had been an attempt on both their parts to shore up their dissolving union, but having the child had not turned an increasingly disastrous marriage into a success.

The problem had been, quite simply, Barbara's possessiveness. She smothered him, resented even his hobbies, hated his magazine plans, and accused him repeatedly of infidelity. It wasn't long before he *had* been unfaithful. When they finally parted she had been bitter and hostile; he had merely been very, very weary.

He had never married again, had never wanted to give another woman the chance to exercise such possessiveness again. But he had known many women over the years. And he knew his own attractiveness to women very well.

Cecelia was different. She was so young, so obviously unawakened. He had always had a connois-

seur's eye for beauty and quality. In Cecelia he
saw something very lovely and very rare. She drove
back with him and Jennifer after the horse show
was over, and as he drove home with his daughter
after dropping Cecelia at Hilltop Farm, he made
the decision that he wanted her.

Chapter Four

On the Wednesday following the horse show Gil had attended, Ricardo Vargas was hospitalized. He had had a persistent cough for over two months but he steadfastly refused to go to the doctor. On Wednesday he experienced difficulty in breathing and finally he allowed Cecelia to drive him to see their family physician. Dr. Harris immediately put him in the hospital.

They put him on oxygen, and as the day progressed his condition seemed to worsen. He was in the town hospital, which was by no means a large medical center, and Dr. Harris wanted him moved. He also wanted a chest specialist to look at him. But there was one problem. Ricardo had no medical coverage. His Blue Cross policy had run out in December and he had not renewed it.

Cecelia was frantic. The personnel at the hospital were firm. They would give Ricardo the best care they could, but under the circumstances, what she was asking for was impossible.

He had been admitted at ten in the morning. At four o'clock Jennifer Archer and Frank Ross arrived. Cecelia was with her father and did not see them; Dr. Harris did.

As she sat and watched her father's face through the oxygen tent Cecelia realized she had never felt more alone in her life. He was all the family she had; there was no one else to turn to. Her mother had been an only child; her father's family were all in Argentina. He was all she had. And she was all *he* had. She had to do something to help him.

A nurse came into the room and said softly, "You have a telephone call, Miss Vargas. It's important."

Numbly Cecelia followed her out to the desk. "Hello?" she said into the receiver.

"Cecelia? It's Gil."

"Gil," she repeated, and some of the numbness lifted.

"Jen called and told me about your father," came the deeply beautiful voice over the wire. "Listen, baby, I've got it all arranged. An ambulance is going to take him into New York—to Mount Sinai. Dr. Stein, one of the best chest specialists in the world, is waiting to look at him. I've talked to him. I've talked to both hospitals. Okay?"

"Oh, thank God," she breathed. Then, more strongly, "Yes, yes, Gil. Okay."

"I'm in Washington but I'm leaving now to fly up to New York. I'll see you at the hospital. Go in with your father in the ambulance."

"Yes, yes I will."

"I'll see you in a few hours then. Chin up, baby." And the line clicked before she even had the chance to say thank you.

*   *   *

The ride into the hospital, with the sirens going all the way, was like a nightmare. Dr. Stein, a big man with a hearty-looking face, was indeed waiting for them. Ricardo was rolled briskly away down a long, long corridor and a nurse put her arm around Cecelia and led her to a book-lined study rich with leather and polished wood where she was settled in a large armchair. "Dr. Stein will see you after he has examined your father, Miss Vargas," the nurse said kindly. "Would you like something to eat? A cup of coffee?"

"Coffee would be fine, if you don't mind," replied Cecelia.

"It will be no trouble," the nurse assured her. "I'll be right back."

After the nurse had left, Cecelia slumped down in the chair and stretched her legs in front of her. She was wearing the same clothes she had put on this morning when she had taken her father directly from the barn to the doctor. She was, however, completely unconscious of the incongruity between her old jeans, sweater, and rubber moccasins and her present expensive surroundings.

The nurse returned with coffee. Cecelia sipped it and waited. It was well over an hour before Dr. Stein appeared. By that time Cecelia was pacing the floor.

"He's all right for the moment," the doctor said immediately. "We have him on oxygen and he's being closely monitored. Please sit down, Miss Vargas."

She perched on the edge of a leather armchair. "But what *is* it, doctor? What is wrong?"

"I don't know," he replied gravely. "His lungs

are functioning at way below their normal level.
I'm going to have to go in to see what is causing
the problem."

"Do you mean—operate?" Cecelia's words were
a mere breath, scarcely a whisper.

"Yes, I'm afraid so," Dr. Stein was saying when
the door opened and a tall blond man appeared
on the threshold.

"Gil!" cried Cecelia and, operating purely on
instinct, leaped out of her chair and ran to him.
His arms opened to enfold her.

"How are you, Gil?" asked Dr. Stein, and Gil,
still keeping one arm around Cecelia, walked over
to where the doctor was standing. He held out his
hand.

"Fine. How are you, Andy? And—more impor-
tantly—how is Cecelia's father?"

The two men exchanged a firm handshake and
Dr. Stein replied, "We have him stabilized at the
moment, but I don't know what is causing the
lungs to fail. I have him scheduled for the operating room at eight o'clock tomorrow morning."

"He'll be all right?" put in Cecelia's fearful voice.

"At the moment he's in our pulmonary intensive care unit," said Dr. Stein reassuringly. "All
the staff there are specially trained. But as to what
the prognosis is—I can't tell you, Miss Vargas. I'll
have to see the lungs first."

"I take it there's nothing we can do around here
tonight, then?" asked Gil.

"No. Mr. Vargas is sleeping at the moment." Dr.
Stein looked at Cecelia. "You need some rest
yourself, young lady. You look exhausted."

"I'll see to it she gets some," said Gil flatly. "We'll be back tomorrow morning, then."

"Right. I'll talk to you as soon as I can."

Once more Gil held out his hand. "Andy, thank you."

"Don't be silly," the big doctor replied.

After he had left the room, Gil turned to Cecelia. "You heard what the doctor said. You need to get some rest." He looked closely into her face. "Have you eaten anything today?"

"No," she replied faintly. "But I'm not hungry."

"Nevertheless, you are going to eat." His tone was peremptory and proprietary and he began to guide her out of the room. "You can spend the night at my apartment on East Seventieth Street," he went on. "It will make getting to the hospital in the morning much easier."

At that she raised her head to look at him. "Gil, how can I ever thank you for all you're doing?"

"To quote Andy," he replied briskly, " 'don't be silly.' Now come on. How about a hamburger?"

They had hamburgers in a small bar near his apartment, and Cecelia found she was hungry after all. At his apartment he showed her into the spare bedroom, handed her a shirt of his own to wear as a nightgown, provided her further with a toothbrush and comb, and wished her good night.

She didn't think she would sleep a wink, but in fact she slept deeply and dreamlessly and woke to Gil's hand on her shoulder. The sun was coming in through the slatted blinds and she blinked sleep out of her eyes as she looked up at him. Memory returned and she sat up abruptly. "What time is it?" she demanded.

"It's eight," he replied calmly. "There's no great rush, Cecelia. The operation is going to take some time. Why don't you get dressed and we'll have some breakfast and then go over to the hospital."

He was dressed already she saw, in twill pants and a navy V-neck sweater. Her hair was streaming across her face and she pushed it away and managed a smile. "Okay."

The operation was long. It was almost noon when Dr. Stein appeared in the study—which, Cecelia had discovered, belonged to the director of the hospital. The name "Gilbert Archer" had clout.

"The lungs were covered with scar tissue—it was blocking proper respiration," Dr. Stein said immediately. "I cleared them up as best I could, but there has been some permanent damage done. How much remains to be seen."

"Scar tissue?" said Cecelia blankly.

"Yes. Evidently he has been walking around with some disease that has been systematically eating away at his lungs. I've sent tissue samples to the lab but if I had to make a guess I'd say he's had pneumonia."

"Pneumonia? But how could he have pneumonia and not know it?" asked Cecelia.

"It happens all the time. That's why it can be so dangerous." Dr. Stein looked with disapproval at the full ashtray next to Gil's chair. "I might add, Miss Vargas," he went on coolly, "that if your father had been a smoker he would most probably be dead by now."

Gil quirked an ironic eyebrow but didn't respond to the implied criticism. Instead he said, "But he will be all right?"

"Yes. As I said, he is going to have some kind of disability, but it shouldn't be life threatening."

"Thank God," said Cecelia fervently.

"Yes," replied Dr. Stein gravely. "He should have seen a doctor much sooner."

"I know. I tried. When can I see him, doctor?"

"He's still in the recovery room. Why don't you come back this evening? He should be back in the intensive care unit by then."

"All right." Cecelia repeated Gil's question. "He's going to be all right?"

"Barring any unforeseen complications—yes."

Cecelia heaved a huge sigh. "I feel like a weight has fallen off my own chest," she confided to the two men. "I don't think I could bear it if I lost Daddy."

"You won't lose him," Gil said. "He couldn't be in better hands."

Cecelia smiled at the lung specialist. "I don't know how to thank you, Dr. Stein. He was dying when we brought him in here—I know he was. You saved his life."

"His own excellent physical condition was his savior, not I," the doctor replied after an almost imperceptible pause. He looked from Cecelia's upturned face to Gil's. "I'm always happy to be of service to a friend of Gil's," he added in a carefully expressionless voice. Gil gave him a pleasant smile in return, but said nothing.

* * *

Gil drove her back to Connecticut, where she packed a suitcase and made arrangements for the horses to be cared for. He then drove her back to New York, fed her, and took her to see her father. They went home to his apartment to sleep.

Cecelia stayed with him for four days, until her father was actually up and walking. He was still in the intensive care unit, but it was clear he was making excellent progress. During the whole time she never once asked herself why Gil was acting as he was, never once questioned the strangeness of his behavior. She knew him scarcely at all and yet she felt she had known him forever. He was there, a rock of strength for her to lean on, and she was grateful. She needed him.

The financial aspects of Gil's assistance would have begun to worry her before long, but Ricardo was before her in the matter. Four days after his operation he asked to see Gil alone. It was evening and Gil had accompanied Cecelia to the hospital. "Go outside for a little, *niña*," Ricardo said gently. "I wish to speak to Mr. Archer."

Cecelia smiled at him. She thought he wanted to thank Gil in private. "All right, Daddy," she agreed, and Ricardo watched her slim figure move gracefully out the door. Gil watched the man in the bed a little warily. Ricardo had lost weight and his normally olive skin had a sallow cast to it, but the dark eyes that looked up at Gil were hard and assessing. In a hospital bed, hooked up to a machine, he still managed to look formidable.

"I wish first of all to thank you for your assistance during my illness," he began formally. "Cecelia tells me it is through your efforts that I was brought to this hospital and Dr. Stein was called in."

"Yes," Gil replied directly. "Cecelia was frantic about you. How did you ever do something as stupid as allowing your coverage to lapse?"

"I have had coverage for over twenty years," Ricardo replied a little bitterly, "and never used it. I put out a lot of money in December on a horse for Cecelia, and when the Blue Cross bill came in I didn't have the cash. I did not intend to drop it permanently, but before I could pay it up—this happened."

Gil remembered the big chestnut in the barn at Hilltop Farm and Cecelia's comment that he was her new jumper. "I see," he said noncommittally.

Ricardo was regarding him very gravely, his brown eyes unwavering on Gil's face. "Under the circumstances, Mr. Archer," he said soberly, "I must ask you what your intentions are in regard to my daughter."

It was a question straight out of the nineteenth century, and coming from this man Gil found it not at all strange. His answer was equally old-fashioned. "I would like to marry her, Señor Vargas," he said formally. "Do I have your permission?"

There was a long silence as two pairs of eyes, dark and light, assessed each other. "Cecelia is not as other girls her age," Ricardo said finally.

"I realize that. I will take good care of her, I promise you."

Very, very slowly Ricardo nodded. "Yes. You are a man. Too many *norteamericanos* are boys—

and a boy would not do for Cecelia. I think you will make her happy."

"I will certainly do my best," Gil said. "I may speak to her, then?"

"Yes," replied Ricardo Vargas. "You may speak to her."

Gil smiled a little. "Thank you, Señor Vargas."

Money was not mentioned between them then or at any time in the future. Both knew that Gil would pay all the hospital bills. But both knew also that if Ricardo had not approved of Gil, he would never have allowed him to address Cecelia. Money was not something that weighed heavily with a man like Ricardo Vargas.

In the minds of both Ricardo and Gil, Cecelia's response was a foregone conclusion. Gil knew she liked him, trusted him, was indebted to him. Ricardo knew the same. Of course Cecelia would say yes.

She didn't say yes immediately. She was too stunned. "You want to marry *me*?" she asked, incredulity in her rising voice.

"I want to marry you," he returned gravely, looking down into her upturned face. They were both standing in her kitchen; he had come in with her after driving her home from the hospital.

She put her hand on the back of one of the kitchen chairs for support and said, bewilderedly, "But why? You—why, you could marry anyone you wanted to. Why me? I don't understand."

He smiled a little crookedly. "Cecelia," he said on a breath of laughter, "you are just too good to be true." And then he put his hands on her shoulders and pulled her toward him. With unhurried leisure he bent his head and began to kiss her.

Cecelia had been kissed before—kissed far more often than her father had ever dreamed—but this time the kissing was being done by an expert. It made quite a difference. She swayed against him, and after a minute her arms went up to circle his neck. When the pressure of his mouth on hers increased she parted her lips for him and felt his arms tighten to hold her even closer. It was a shock when he let her go and she stood for a minute in the circle of his arm, blinking up at him out of enormous dark eyes.

He reached a hand up and gently touched her rose-flushed cheek. "That is why I want to marry you," he said a trifle unsteadily.

"Oh," breathed Cecelia.

"Well?" he asked, and his voice had regained its normal tone. It held once again the hint of amusement that was so familiar to her now. "What do you say?"

It still didn't seem possible to her that this was happening. That this man, this godlike being, should be asking to marry *her*. As she still stared at him in incredulous wonder he said, "I have your father's permission, if that means something."

"You asked Daddy?" she queried in astonishment.

"Yes." He looked down into her perfect oval face with its beautifully planed cheekbones, delicate nose, and large luminous eyes. His own eyes began to take on a smoky hue. "This afternoon, when you left us alone," he added.

"I see." Her eyes were caught now in his. His lashes were much darker than his hair, she noticed inconsequentially. "I'd like to marry you very much, Gil," she finally said in a small voice to the daunting creature in front of her.

He smiled. "That makes me very happy, baby. And Jennifer will be happy, too," he added, because he thought she'd like to hear that.

"I hope so," said Cecelia a little wistfully.

"How about fixing us some coffee and we can plot the future?" he suggested.

"Okay," replied Cecelia and obediently moved to the stove.

It was not until quite a while after he had left that Cecelia's amazement wore off and a little unease began to creep in. Gil, she reflected a little sadly, had never once said he loved her.

Chapter Five

❧

Ricardo Vargas left the hospital two weeks after he was operated on and went to a very exclusive convalescent home in Arizona where he was to stay for a month. The morning of his departure Gil and Cecelia were married.

Everything had happened to her so quickly that Cecelia felt events to be quite beyond her control. Gil said he had been neglecting his work shamefully, that he could take a week off for a honeymoon if they were married at the beginning of June, but once they got into the summer he would be tied up. Ricardo seemed to feel that a quick marriage was a good idea as well; he did not like the idea of leaving her alone.

So on a sunny morning in early June they were married. They saw Ricardo safely off on a plane to Arizona and then they themselves boarded a plane for Nassau. A friend of Gil's was lending them his home on Paradise Island for their honeymoon.

The house was fabulous and fully staffed with servants. It was set on the water with its own

private beach, a boat, and a beautiful pool as well.
Gil had visited it many times and he undertook to
show her around.

Cecelia felt rather as if she were living in a
dream. They had dinner in the beautiful glass-
enclosed, air-conditioned dining room, served by
silent-footed and efficient servants. Cecelia was
not aware of what it was she ate. Her mind was on
Gil and what was to come afterward, upstairs in
their bedroom.

She was afraid. Not for herself—she was not so
Victorian as all that. She was afraid that she would
disappoint him. It seemed to her, from all the sex
manuals she had seen crowding the shelves of
bookstores, that to be good at making love was
quite a complicated business. If entire books had
been written about the procedure, it obviously was
far from simple. Gil was a man of the world. She
was afraid he was going to expect more from her
than he was likely to get.

When they went upstairs together to the bedroom after dinner she tried to tell him something
of what she was feeling. It had grown dark outside and he went over to the window to draw the
drapes. She stood in the center of the large yellow
and green room watching his tall figure silhouet-
ted against the grass-green drapes. He turned to
look at her and she said, hesitantly, "Gil . . ."

"Yes?" He smiled encouragingly and began to
cross the room toward her. She had put on a
turquoise sundress for dinner and his eyes were
on her bare throat and shoulders. He seemed so
tall to her, so gleaming in his blondness.

"I think I ought to explain that I've never done

this before," she said in a low voice. She couldn't meet his eyes and looked instead at his tie. It was a very attractive tie, navy blue with a discreet stripe. It matched the navy blazer he had worn for dinner. The blazer now reposed on a yellow chair, where Gil had tossed it when they entered the room. He had opened the top button of his collar as well and loosened the tie she was regarding with such fascination.

"Is that so?" he asked, and she could hear the laughter in his voice. "I would never have guessed."

At that she did look up at him. There was laughter in his eyes as well. Her lips curled a little at the corners. "I'm dreadfully ignorant," she confessed. "I hope you're not going to be disappointed."

The laughter abruptly left his eyes and they narrowed. "You couldn't possibly disappoint me, baby," he murmured, and putting his hands on her shoulders, he gently drew her closer. Then he bent his head and kissed her.

He had kissed her during the last two weeks, but never again as he had done when he asked her to marry him. And never like this. He held her so tightly that she could feel the whole length of his hard lean body pressed against hers. His mouth moved on her and she answered his demand, her own lips parting. His hold on her loosened and she could feel one of his hands sliding up the smooth length of her arm to caress her bare shoulder. The feel of his hand was exquisite and she felt herself melting under his touch, her mouth now moving in response to his own. He brushed the strap of her sundress aside and his hand slid under the bodice and touched her breast. Cecelia was swamped with the sensations he aroused.

His mouth moved away from hers and across her cheek. Her hair was swept back into a chignon and he kissed her exposed ear. "Baby," he whispered, "you don't need to know a thing. I'll teach you."

His hand was still on her breast, moving caressingly, setting fire to all her insides. "Gil," she whispered raggedly.

His other hand was in her hair, pulling out pins and scattering them all over the floor. "I've wanted you for so long," he murmured, and she could hear the thickness in his voice. "So long. My beautiful Cecelia." Her hair was down now and his hand moved to the zipper on her dress. He had it down in a minute and slid it off her so that it fell to the floor, leaving her clad only in her panties and half-slip, her long dark hair streaming over her naked shoulders and halfway down her back. She shivered under his gaze and he bent, without touching her, and kissed her again. Cecelia's lips parted immediately and his tongue traced a delicate circle inside her mouth, as all the while he was unbuttoning his own shirt. When he finished he raised his head and said in a husky voice, "Let's go to bed."

By this time Cecelia would have done anything he suggested. "All right," she whispered and he picked her up and carried her over to the big king-size bed. The maid had already turned the covers back and the sheets felt smooth and cool under her as he laid her down. When he slid her remaining clothes off her, her breath caught in her throat, but not from fear. She stared at him in wonder as he shed his own clothes, and as he came to her on the bed she thought that he was indeed like the god she had thought him: strong and lean and beautiful.

Making love proved to be a far less complicated process than Cecelia had imagined. In fact, nothing had ever come to her more naturally than knowing how to respond to Gil. As he touched and caressed her, as he kissed her all over and whispered love words to her, she lost all sense of her own separate identity. As he took her to where she had never been before and as the wonder of it shook her body with shuddering waves of pleasure, the whole world receded, leaving only this one man. He filled the universe and whatever he wanted from her he could have.

It was a very long time before she opened her eyes again. When finally she did she found him looking down into her face. He looked very grave. She looked back at him, her own eyes soft and very very dark. "Cecelia," he said, and lightly touched her mouth with his forefinger. There was a note almost of wonder in his voice.

There was only one thing she could say to him now. "I love you."

A small smile pulled at the corners of his mouth but his eyes remained grave. "My love," he said. "I certainly hope so." At that she smiled at him, radiant, her face framed on the pillow by the spilled mass of her hair. His mouth quirked a little and then he reached down to pull the blankets up over them. The air conditioning was beginning to feel cool on their heated bodies. "Let's get some sleep," he said softly. "You must be tired. You've had a long day."

"It was a lovely day, though," she replied and then, obediently, settled down into her pillow and closed her eyes. He watched her for a moment longer before he turned off the light.

She awoke early the following morning and lay perfectly still beside him in the bed, savoring the feel of her own happiness. He was sleeping on his side with his back toward her and the sight of that well-muscled brown back did strange things to her insides. For all his leanness, she thought, he was whipcord strong. The thought struck her that she had met him for the first time only two months ago. Whoever would have dreamed, when she had first looked over to see him standing in the doorway of her arena, that they would end up like this?

Suddenly, his large frame twitched, and she watched the play of muscles as he turned toward her. "What's so funny?" inquired a deep voice somewhere next to her right ear. She turned her head on the pillow to look up at his face.

"I was just thinking about the first time I met you," she explained, her lips still curved in a smile.

"Oh? And what did you think of me when you first met me?"

"I thought you were very handsome," she confessed a little mischievously. "I had seen pictures of you in the paper but the reality was much more impressive."

He grinned at her. "I'm glad to hear that. And

here I was thinking I had to rely on Jennifer to get you to go out with me."

She looked surprised. "Oh. Do you mean you *wanted* to take me out that first time?"

"Cecelia, you are too innocent and modest to be let out alone," he said humorously. "It's a damn good thing you've got yourself a husband to keep an eye on you."

Her brow was furrowed. "I don't know what you mean."

He regarded her for some seconds in silence. She was so unaware of her own beauty, so undemanding of attention; he had always found it difficult to account for. He said now, curiously, "Didn't all the boys you knew pursue you for dates?"

"Of course not," she said promptly. "I don't mean I was a wallflower," she added, "but, much as I hate to shatter your highly flattering assumption, neither was I the belle of the ball."

"That's astonishing," he murmured and she grinned.

"Well, if I'm the belle of *your* ball, that's all I care about."

He smiled back a little absently, his thoughts elsewhere. "You are, baby," he said in reply to her comment. He looked at the face on the pillow next to him and tried to comprehend what she had just told him. He reached out and gently touched one exquisite cheekbone. It was true, he thought, that her beauty wasn't the vapid kind one found gracing magazine or television commercials. There was character in Cecelia's face. And intelligence. Hers was not the sort of face that would be picked to sell California sunshine.

Hers was the sort of face that had launched a
thousand ships on Troy. He supposed the boys
her age were too young to see that. She was looking at him a little questioningly and he said, "How
about a before-breakfast swim?"

Cecelia had rather hoped he might have other
ideas but she smothered her disappointment and
said agreeably, "Okay. Sounds like fun."

Their bedroom windows were really sliding-glass
doors that led out to a patio and then down a few
steps to the beach. And it was to the beach and
not to the pool they went a few minutes later, Gil
clad in blue bathing trunks and Cecelia in a new
hot-pink suit she had bought for her honeymoon.
They dropped their towels down on the fine white
sand and ran, laughing, into the clear green water.

They swam and splashed each other and swam
again for about a half hour before they came out
and retrieved their towels from the beach. "Let's
take a walk before we go in," Gil suggested. "There's
a spot of beach I want to show you."

She fell into step with him companionably, walking hand in hand along the edge of the water.
They made a striking couple, the tall fair-haired
man and the slender dark girl beside him. They
rounded a curve of beach and came to what was a
little cove. Palm trees grew nearly down to the
water. "It's lovely, Gil," Cecelia said sincerely.

"Isn't it? It belongs to Jim as well. And it's
completely private—we'll be quite undisturbed."

"What do you mean?" she faltered, watching
him carefully spread out their towels on the sand.

He straightened from his task with the ease and
grace of an eighteen-year-old. Coming over to her

he slid the straps of her bathing suit off her shoulders. Her eyes widened in shock. "You can't mean . . . ?"

"Oh, but I do," he murmured and bent to kiss the smoothness of her shoulders. The touch of his mouth sent shivers all along her spine. "This is a very nice bathing suit," he was saying, "but I think we can dispense with it for the moment." It was down now to her waist. "Kiss me, Cecelia," he said softly, and as if in a trance, she raised her mouth to his. When his lips touched hers a flame of response ran all through her. His hands were moving slowly over her bared upper body, and an exquisite ache began to grow deep inside her. When he took his mouth away from hers and whispered, "Lie down for me, baby," she made no sound of protest. Instead she finished taking off her suit and lay down on the spread towels, feeling the warmth of the morning sun on her bare flesh, stretching out to give him access to all of her lovely young body.

"Gil," she whispered, as he shed his own suit and lay down beside her. "Ah, Gil."

He took his time as the sun rose higher and higher in the sky and Cecelia's passion rose higher and higher with it, until she was drowning in sensation, wanting him as she had not thought it possible for a woman ever to want. The explosion of pleasure, when it finally came, was shattering, and she clung to the man who was able to do this to her, her body totally delivered up to his own desire, the two of them hurtling together through the profound depths and heights of physical love.

*   *   *

For Cecelia her honeymoon was the opening of a door onto another world. She had been remarkably insulated from the sexual fever that permeated so much of the modern world. Ricardo had kept her a child for much longer than was usual in the United States. In regard to his daughter he was very much a Latin male. Cecelia's world had revolved for many years solely around her father, the horses, and school. She had dated occasionally once she reached the age of seventeen, but no boy had ever made much of an impression on her, nor had their kisses ever raised her pulse by even one extra beat.

And then Gil came into her life. She realized in retrospect that she had been physically attracted to him ever since she had first met him. She had been, she thought in rueful amusement, too dumb to recognize the signs. She knew now. She knew what it was to be part of a man, to hunger for him, to be made happy merely by his glance, his smile. Before her marriage she had thought him wonderful, a chevalier on a white horse who had rescued the maiden in distress. He had been above her, beyond her, unreachable. He was that no longer. He was her husband, wedded to her by an intimacy of intense passion she had not suspected could exist between two people.

She watched him one afternoon, unnoticed, from the shadow of the pool chaise longue. He had gone into Nassau to see someone in the government and had been gone all morning. She had heard the car door slam and turned to watch him as he came around the side of the house, his head bent a little in thought. The bright tropical sun struck sparks of silver from his thick smooth hair. She thought suddenly, with an ache in her heart, how much he meant to her. All her life was there, walking toward her in the hot sun. She swallowed, waited a minute, and then called, "How did it go?"

He crossed the patio to the pool and sat down on the edge of her chaise. "Nothing much new. I thought I'd better go, though, since he wanted to see me. It's always a good idea to keep ministers well disposed toward one."

"Yes," she said. "Someday there *might* be something new."

He grinned. "Exactly." He reached up and loosened his tie. "God, but it's hot." He was wearing his navy blazer and green sailcloth pants.

"Go get your trunks on and come for a swim," Cecelia suggested. "That'll cool you off."

"Mmm." He didn't rise right away, however, but looked instead at the book that was resting on her bare brown thigh. "What's that you're reading?" he asked. The book was in Spanish.

"It's a new novel by a Peruvian author I particularly like," she answered, holding it up for him to see.

"Do you like Latin American writing?" His expression was hidden behind his sunglasses.

"Most of it," she replied. "I especially like Llosa. He can be very funny."

He nodded thoughtfully. "I've never read him. I'll have to give him a try. In English, I hasten to add." He rose. "I think I'll take your advice about a swim." She smiled up at him without replying and he bent to lightly kiss her mouth. "You look good enough to eat," he murmured. "I think that later I'll do just that."

She watched him as he walked back toward the house, her mouth very soft and tender. She loved him so much. She hated the thought of having to go home.

Chapter Six

They flew home first-class on a regularly scheduled flight, only to find a collection of photographers and newsmen waiting for them in New York. Cecelia was utterly astonished to find that her marriage was a news item.

Gil paused for a few minutes to answer questions and Cecelia stood as close to him as she could. "Look this way, Mrs. Archer!" someone called. She looked and a flash went off. She jumped a little in surprise and Gil glanced down at her and then put a hand on her arm.

"That's all for now, ladies and gentlemen," he said pleasantly, and with a firm hand he began to steer her across the lounge. Frank was waiting with the car and Cecelia gratefully got in and sank back against the cushions.

"Sorry about that," Gil said as the car started up and moved away. "I'll get a press release out tomorrow and that should satisfy the gossip mongers."

"I hope so," said Cecelia doubtfully. It had just occurred to her that she knew nothing whatever of Gil's world. She had never seen him in his own milieu, only in hers. She had never met his friends, his business associates, his professional and social acquaintances. It was an aspect of marriage to him that she had not yet had a chance to consider, the fact that he belonged to a world vastly different from the world she was accustomed to. All during her father's illness, and then on their honeymoon, there had been just the two of them. She realized now that, childishly, she had somehow thought that that's what it would continue to be, with only the added—and welcome—addition of Jennifer. She had a sinking feeling, as she listened to him question Frank closely about people she did not know, that her honeymoon was over.

As they turned into the driveway of Gil's home the uneasiness that had been building inside Cecelia during the ride intensified. She had been to The Birches before, but it seemed now that she was seeing it with new eyes. What would it mean, she thought, to be mistress of such a house?

Her new home was a beautiful stone Georgian manor house set well back from the road and surrounded by manicured lawns and old trees. Gil had shown her the entire house before they were married and introduced her to the small army of daily servants who saw to the upkeep of the grounds and the house. The inside of the house was as graciously lovely as the exterior. On the first floor there were a large living room, a banquet-sized dining room, a breakfast room that served as the family dining room, a morning room with French doors opening to a flagstone patio, and an oak-paneled library. Upstairs were seven enormous bedrooms and baths. There was a separate servants wing, where the Rosses lived. And on the grounds there were a beautifully landscaped pool and a Har-tru tennis court.

They came into the large central hall, both Gil and Frank carrying suitcases. There was the sound of hurried steps on the stairs and then Jennifer appeared. "Daddy!" she cried and ran across the hall to throw herself into his arms. Gil dropped the suitcase he was holding to swing her up off the floor for a minute.

"What are you doing home from school?" he asked with mock severity.

She glowed up at him. "Nora said I could stay home today to be your welcoming party." She turned to Cecelia and hesitated, looking a little shy. Cecelia held out her arms and the little girl hugged her fiercely. Over her silvery curls Cecelia's eyes met Gil's; there was a faint smile on his lips and tenderness in his light gray eyes.

When Jennifer stepped back Cecelia said to her, "I'm dying to hear about my horses. What's been going on? Is everything okay?"

"Yes. Miss Rice has been terrific," Jennifer responded. "Gucci has a swollen nose, though, and Lady is still sore. . . ." Jennifer was a mine of information and chattered all the way upstairs and then back down again as they went into the breakfast room to have lunch. Gil's eyes glinted with amusement as he listened to his wife and daughter but he made no move to interrupt a conversation they both apparently found fascinating.

Cecelia's honeymoon ended abruptly at two o'clock that afternoon with a telephone call. Gil came back from the library where he had taken it, his fair brows knitted together. "That was Hank at the office," he told Cecelia. "Trouble is brewing in the Middle East. I'm going into the office for a while."

"All right," Cecelia answered composedly. "Will we see you for dinner?"

"I don't know," he answered. His frown had lifted and he looked very alert. "I'll call you."

"All right," she answered again and raised her face for his kiss.

He tousled Jennifer's curls absently, said, "I'm taking Frank. If you want to go over to the farm use the wagon," and was on his way. He looked, Cecelia thought a little sadly, extremely happy to be back in harness once again.

She and Jennifer went over to Hilltop Farm that afternoon and Cecelia soon was as absorbed in her job as Gil in his. The riding school had been in suspension for over a month, ever since Ricardo had been hospitalized, and Cecelia plunged into plans to start it up again. She would have to do all the teaching until her father was home.

Cecelia and Jennifer returned to The Birches for dinner and Nora told Cecelia that Gil had called to say he wouldn't be home. "Daddy's hardly ever home for dinner," Jennifer confided.

"Oh?" Cecelia hoped her voice did not betray her feelings. "Well, I expect he's very busy at the magazine," she added carefully.

"Yes, he is," replied Jennifer vigorously. "That's why I'm so glad he married you. It won't be so lonely, now that you're here, Cecelia."

"No," said Cecelia a little forlornly. "It won't be lonely."

She spent the evening on the telephone, calling her students and her father's students and setting up a new teaching schedule. She had a lot of hard work ahead of her, she realized as she looked at her red appointment book. Not only did she have lessons all week but she had to organize all the weekend trips to shows as well. Ricardo had several junior riders who were collecting an impressive number of points, and one of the girls was a sure Maclay finalist. Filling in for her father was going to be one big job.

She was in bed and almost asleep when Gil finally came home. "How did it go?" she asked foggily when she heard him come into the bedroom.

"All right," he answered. He bent to kiss her cheek; it was warm with sleep. "I didn't mean to wake you, baby," he said softly.

"That's all right," she answered. "I wasn't asleep." He went into the bathroom and by the time he came back, she was.

The alarm rang the next morning at 5:45. Gil rolled over and turned it off. "A quarter to six?" he said, peering sleepily at the dial.

"I'm afraid so." Cecelia swung her legs out of bed, already alert, as she usually was in the morning. "Horses breakfast early," she told her husband. "I'll reset the clock for you. What time do you get up?"

"Seven," he answered definitely. She reset the clock and bent down to kiss his ruffled hair. She dressed quietly in dungarees and a pink Izod shirt. He was sleeping again as she left the bedroom and went downstairs to breakfast. They had been home only one day, she thought with dismay, and already they were passing like ships in the night.

Liz Lewis sat in her elegant Manhattan apartment and looked with narrowed eyes at the entry that appeared in the "Notices" section of *News Report:*

> *Married*   Gilbert Archer, 35, owner and editor of *News Report* and Cecelia Vargas, 22, daughter of Argentine equestrian and Olympic gold medalist, Ricardo Vargas; he for the second time, she for the first; in Fairridge, Connecticut.

Liz threw the magazine down, lit a cigarette, and stalked impatiently around her earth-toned living room. After a few minutes she went over to a delicate cherry desk and dialed a number on the telephone. After the conversation had been concluded to her satisfaction she sat down at the desk and, taking out pen and paper, began to compile a list of names. At the top of the list were Mr. and Mrs. Gilbert Archer.

"Whatever can Liz be thinking of?" Pat Carruthers said to her husband as she sat looking at the invitation in her hand. "A party in New York? In the summer?"

"Where is it?" Ben Carruthers reached out and took the invitation from his wife. "The Plaza. And for the Earl of Ashbrook." He raised an impressed eyebrow. "Liz *has* been busy. He's Britain's new UN representative. How ever does she know him?"

"His wife went to school with us," Pat replied simply. "She was Anne Netherfield."

"Ah." He handed her back the card. "Well, I'll bet you anything that Liz gets all acceptances. You know how Americans love a lord."

"I know," replied Pat. "But why, I wonder, didn't Liz wait until September?"

Gilbert Archer was as surprised as the Carruthers when Liz's invitation arrived at The Birches. He did not comment, however, but passed it on to Cecelia with the remark, "We'll have to go. Better put it down on your calendar."

They were having a drink together this Friday evening, one of the rare evenings Gil was home for dinner. Jennifer was upstairs doing her homework and the two of them were alone together in the living room. Cecelia looked up from the invitation and said, "I know Lord Ashbrook is England's new UN representative—I read that in the paper. But who is Liz Lewis?"

He regarded his martini with interest and answered, "A friend of mine. Both our marriages broke up at the same time and we went around together for a bit. She's rather a hotshot hostess type."

"I see," replied Cecelia slowly. And indeed, with her newfound maturity, she did see. Gil was not the sort of man who had platonic friendships with the opposite sex. She felt a sharp pang of jealousy and forced herself to say calmly, "Do you know, I've never met any of your friends?"

At that he turned to look at her. "Well, you'll meet a lot of them at this party, baby." He grinned. "And believe me, they'll be anxious to meet you."

"Oh dear," said Cecelia, half comically, half nervously. Then, "What shall I wear?"

"A gown," he replied positively. He looked at her, head a little to one side. "Why don't you come into New York on Monday and I'll take you shopping."

"That would be lovely," she replied fervently. "You'll know much better than I what's appropriate."

"You have excellent taste in clothes," he said, surveying her with approval. She wore a soft jacquard shirt-dress in a pale garden-flower print and apple-green strappy sandals. Her long dark hair was held off her temples by two tortoise-shell combs and fell, sheer and shining, past her shoulders.

Cecelia smoothed the full skirt over her knee. "Thank you," she said softly, "but I'm sure we dress more casually in Connecticut than is customary in New York."

He smiled at her and held out his hand. "I like the casual look," he told her. "I'd like a more casual life, too. It seems as if I've hardly seen you these past weeks."

It was true. The crisis in the Mid East had blown up as predicted, and Gil had spent most of his waking hours in the office, topped off by a quick trip to Cairo to talk to a source who had proved valuable in the past. Cecelia had missed him terribly. She put her hand in his now and smiled up into his eyes. Those eyes narrowed at her response and took on a heavy-lidded look that she recognized. Her heartbeat accelerated and he made as if to raise her hand to his lips.

Nora appeared in the living room doorway and announced, "Dinner is ready." Gil dropped Cecelia's hand and the two of them walked sedately into the breakfast room where Nora's famous beef burgundy awaited them.

Later that evening, as Cecelia, dressed in a champagne-colored nightgown, was sitting before the lovely antique dressing table that Gil had provided for her, her thoughts went once again to the upcoming party. She regarded her reflection in the mirror critically, frowned, and said over her shoulder to Gil, "Maybe I should get my hair cut. This style isn't very sophisticated." She was still staring at her reflection when he appeared in the mirror behind her; he had taken his shirt off and was wearing only his light blue seersucker trousers. He was still very tanned—he had returned from Egypt only two days ago.

"Cut it and I'll beat you," he said. Her eyes widened in surprise. He slid his hand into the shining thickness of the hair under question and tilted her head back until she was looking up at him. "Your hair is beautiful," he murmured and kissed her upturned mouth. When he raised his head he said softly, "Don't cut it."

"All right," she whispered back, feeling herself melting under the power of his kiss, his voice. His hand moved from her hair down to her bare shoulder and then, bending, he began to kiss the side of her throat.

"Let's go to bed," he murmured.

"All right," Cecelia whispered once again.

On Monday Cecelia went into New York and Gil took her shopping. It was at Saks Fifth Avenue that they bought the gown that she would wear to the upcoming party. It was a white sheath dress by Halston, simple and uncluttered and wickedly sophisticated. It was also outrageously expensive, but Gil didn't seem to mind at all. He took Cecelia out for a delicious lunch and then to Tiffany's, where he bought her a diamond necklace to wear with the gown. Cecelia protested about the money he was spending but he didn't listen. "I like to spend money on you, baby," he said simply.

Gil was as busy as ever during the following week, and Cecelia, even though she was frantically busy as well, felt within herself a growing dissatisfaction with the way their life together was shaping up. It seemed to her as if he had his life and she had hers and the only time the two of them met was in bed.

When her father came home, she thought, then perhaps things would change. Gil knew she was completely tied down at present by the horses and the riding school. When she was freer, then he might find more ways to include her in his own life. Or perhaps, she found herself thinking a little uncomfortably, perhaps he didn't think she would fit in with his life. Perhaps he didn't think she would fit in with his friends. Perhaps he thought she was too young. It suddenly became very important to her that she handle successfully the upcoming party for Lord and Lady Ashbrook. In her mind it began to take on the aura of a test.

Cecelia was not the only person who was regarding the upcoming party in the light of a test. Liz Lewis was a very clever woman as well as a very lovely one. It had come as a nasty shock to discover that Gil had married another woman. It had been equally nasty to discover the age of that other woman. However, upon reflection, it had begun to appear to Liz as if Cecelia's age might work against her in some respects as effectively as it had obviously worked for her in others.

Gil, she decided, had fallen for a pretty face and a supple young body. It surprised her—but then he certainly was not the first man who had been so ensnared. He was not a man, however, who would have much patience with a wife who was socially awkward or who did not fit in with the intelligent, sophisticated, and cultured circle he himself belonged to by reason of birth, ability, and natural charm. A twenty-two-year-old girl who had done nothing all her life but ride horses would not fit in. Of that Liz was positive.

The party at the Plaza, by very reason of its unexpectedness, its novelty, its guest of honor, and its hostess, was rapidly becoming one of the "in" social events of the year. The most brilliant and charming men and women in New York society were coming; the whole affair was to be done in the height of magnificent style. Gilbert Archer's young wife, Liz Lewis thought with complacency, should feel very much out of place.

Chapter Seven

Cecelia spent the morning and afternoon of the day of the party at a horse show. Gil had been annoyed when she said she had to go, but it was an important show and she felt it her responsibility to take the Hilltop Farm Show Team. She also took Czar and collected two blue ribbons herself in the Open Jumper classes.

She got home at five o'clock, in time to eat something, bathe, pack a suitcase—they were staying overnight in the New York apartment—and change into her gown. Gil and Jennifer had spent the day at home, lazing around the pool, and Gil had given Jennifer a tennis lesson. The little girl told Cecelia all about it as she sat on Cecelia's bed and watched her dress. They appeared to have had a very pleasant day together and Cecelia felt badly that she had not been at home. They needed time together as a family, and they seemed to get it so seldom. Whenever Gil managed to be home, she was out.

"You look super, Cecelia," Jenny said, staring in awe at her young stepmother.

Cecelia regarded her own reflection with some satisfaction. The simple halter-top white gown looked very dramatic against the golden tan of her bare arms and shoulders. She had swept her hair back into a style she had seen and admired in a magazine in the dentist's office the previous week when she had taken Jennifer for a checkup. She thought it looked elegant and sophisticated. The diamonds that circled her long slender neck helped immeasurably, she thought. "Thanks," she answered Jenny now. "It's a pretty dress, isn't it?"

"You'll be the prettiest lady there," Jenny assured her, and Cecelia laughed and kissed her good-bye.

"You're prejudiced," she said, "but I appreciate the compliment."

Frank was driving them to the Plaza. He was then going to drop off their suitcases and some groceries at the apartment and return to Connecticut. Gil had said they would get a cab after the party.

Gil didn't say anything when she appeared downstairs; he just escorted her out to the waiting car and held the door for her to get in. Then he got in next to her, Frank slid into the driver's seat, and they were off.

They drove in silence for a little way and then Cecelia said, "Daddy gets home on Tuesday. He's feeling very well, he says. And the doctors say he can take up his teaching schedule again, as long as he doesn't overdo it." It was the only way she could think of to apologize for being away all during the day.

"That's good news," he replied easily.

"Yes." She glanced at him slantwise, thinking how very handsome he looked in his formal evening clothes and wondering whether or not to mention a problem that was bothering her.

"You're going to have to get a woman to come in to cook and clean for him," Gil said, bringing up the subject that had been weighing on her for a week or so. He turned to look at her directly. "I didn't mind your helping out this last month while he's been sick, but I don't want you over there cleaning the house and making his dinner. Find someone reliable to come in and I'll pay her."

She bit her lip. It was the solution she had thought of as well, but somehow, the way he had put it . . . "All right," she said in a low voice. "I'll see if I can find someone."

"No if's," he said firmly. "Find someone. And find someone as well to help out in the barn. This business of your getting up every morning before six to go feed the horses can't continue. You're gone before I even get up. Before *Jennifer* gets up," he added forcefully. "I don't like it."

"It isn't easy to get someone reliable to come in every morning," she said in a low voice.

"Someone did while you were away in Nassau," he pointed out reasonably.

"Yes, that was Marie Rice. But she's a teacher— she only did that as a favor. And the kids all have to be in school. And Daddy definitely should not be forking hay."

"Cecelia," he said very quietly, very pleasantly, "either you find someone to feed those horses or I will."

He had never spoken to her like that before.

She straightened her slim shoulders and lifted her chin. "I'll find someone," she said evenly.

"Good." He smiled at her and changed the subject. "You look terrific. You're going to knock them all dead tonight."

He had gotten her hackles up with his peremptory attitude and now he disarmed her completely with his smile, his look of admiration. "I don't want to knock them dead," she said after a brief pause, "I just want to have a good time."

"You'll do both," he said confidently. As they got out of the car in front of the Plaza, however, Gil found himself suddenly not so sure of how much Cecelia would enjoy the evening. For the first time he realized how awkward she might feel, faced with a large party where she wouldn't know a soul. A large party of people all of whom were not only strangers but also older than she. Liz Lewis's party at the Plaza was a long way from the casual beer and pizza gatherings his young wife was undoubtedly accustomed to. He took her arm as they entered the reception room of the suite, determined to stick with her for the evening.

Liz Lewis and Lord and Lady Ashbrook were receiving their guests. When Liz caught sight of Gil's tall figure in the doorway she felt her heartbeat begin to accelerate. Her eyes went from his silver-blond head to the girl who was beside him.

She had thought Gil's new wife would be smashing. But as Cecelia smiled at her and murmured a pleasantry the thought flashed through Liz's brain that she hadn't been prepared for this. Cecelia Archer was not smashing. She was, quite simply, beautiful. And her beauty had nothing to do with her youth. She would be beautiful when she was eighty. Gil was holding Liz's hand now and she forced a smile. She heard him say something humorous to the Ashbrooks, whom he knew, and then he and his wife moved into the other room.

Twenty minutes later Liz left her post on the reception line and came into the large room where most of her guests were drinking champagne and cocktails. Her searching eye picked out the Archers almost immediately. They were standing together by one of the velvet-draped windows. Cecelia's head was tipped back as she looked up at her husband. He was talking. Suddenly she broke into laughter and Liz saw the instant response on Gil's face. Her lips tightened. Then a man appeared next to Gil and murmured a few words. Gil hesitated, casting a worried look at Cecelia. She smiled at him and said something that must have reassured him for he went off across the room with the man whom Liz recognized, and Cecelia was left standing by herself in front of the window. Liz regarded her isolation with satisfaction. She had no intention of lifting a finger to help the beautiful child-bride out of her obvious predicament.

Cecelia watched Gil go off with a sinking feeling in the pit of her stomach. One of Liz's guests was a former secretary of state whose influence and prestige were enormous. He wanted to talk to Gil, privately, or so the young man who had taken Gil away had said. She had seen the worried look Gil had thrown her and had sent him off with a determinedly serene smile, but she felt anything but serene as she surveyed the glittering crowd before her. Gil had introduced her to a number of people, but Cecelia could not see any of them at just that moment.

She felt utterly miserable. She longed to put down her champagne glass and just walk out the door. But of course she couldn't do that. She had to stay and pretend she felt easy and happy and carefree. She was raising her glass to take another sip of champagne when she heard a voice call, "Cecelia!" She turned and saw a gray-haired woman dressed in blue coming toward her through the crowd. Cecelia broke into a delighted smile.

"Maisie! What a surprise to see you!"

"Nothing like as big a surprise as you gave us, honey. I couldn't believe it when I read the papers. And how is your father?"

"He's fine, Maisie. He's been convalescing in Arizona, but he'll be home on Tuesday."

"I'm glad to hear that." She frowned. "I hope his hunting days aren't over?" Maisie Winter was charter member of the Ridgeview Hunt—which was where Cecelia knew her from. Maisie's husband—a fact Cecelia had not known—was president of a New York bank.

"I hope not too," Cecelia said fervently.

"So tell me now," Maisie said curiously, "however did you come to marry Gil Archer?"

Cecelia grinned. "He asked me."

Maisie broke into laughter. "I see." She spotted someone across the room and raised the voice that could be heard across half a mile on the hunting field. "George! Here's Cecelia!"

"My heavens." A burly man with thinning red hair arrived to beam at her. "Cecelia, my dear, how lovely to see you. And how is Ricardo?" George was another member of Cecelia's hunt. She had known him since she was nine.

The three of them were talking and laughing comfortably when they were joined by a tall, distinguished-looking man of about fifty-five. He was, Cecelia learned afterward, president of the largest brokerage house on Wall Street. He came over and took her hand, saying, "I know you, young lady, although you don't know me. My daughter Nancy rode in the Maclay Cup finals in nineteen seventy-five, seventy-six, and seventy-seven. She was third once and second twice. A certain Cecelia Vargas was first all those times—unfortunately."

Cecelia's large eyes widened. "Are you Nancy Clark's father?"

"I am," he said.

Cecelia smiled. "How do you do?" she said. "How *is* Nancy? I thought she was going to ride for the USET?"

When Gil emerged almost an hour later from a very interesting conversation with the ex-secretary of state, he looked immediately for his wife. He located her after a minute in the middle of a large, animated group that included two bank presidents and their wives, two princes of Wall Street, and the Irish ambassador to the United States.

Liz Lewis was not enjoying herself. She had had no idea that several of her most distinguished guests had evidently known Cecelia from her childhood. Liz's clever plan was going most sadly awry.

Gil was surprised to find his wife so evidently

known as well, but for him the surprise was a pleasant one. He had always regarded Cecelia's riding as essentially frivolous and occasionally a nuisance; he was consequently amazed to find her something of a celebrity among many of his peers. "This little gal took the Maclay Cup three years in a row," Glen Clark said to him as Gil joined the group, shaking his head in mock disapproval. "Robbed my poor Nancy, she did."

"What," asked Gil simply, "is the Maclay Cup?"

A whole circle of shocked eyes stared at him. "It's awarded at the National Horse Show to the best junior rider," Cecelia said, her eyes dancing.

"Oh." He looked at her. "And you won it three times?"

"Yes." She evidently found his ignorance very funny.

"All the junior riders of America heaved a sigh of relief when Cecelia turned eighteen," said Glen Clark. "Too bad Nancy wasn't a year younger."

"Too bad Cecelia couldn't ride for the USET," said Mark Evans. He was president of the United States Equestrian Team. "I understand from Roderick that Czar is marvelous," he went on. "Are you going to be at Harrisburg this fall?"

Cecelia glanced at Gil. "I'm not sure," she said. "But Roderick's right, Czar is marvelous. He took two blues today."

"Oh, were you at Ridge Haven today?" asked Mark. "How was . . ." The conversation went enthusiastically on, with Gil listening in growing amazement. He had always thought of himself as a well-rounded person, but this was an area he did not know at all.

Gil and Cecelia were among the first guests to leave the party. At about one o'clock Cecelia began to feel very tired, although she gallantly tried not to show it. Gil had not been pleased when she got up at five o'clock this morning. She was talking to her hostess and Lord Ashbrook when Gil came over to stand behind her. He said a few things to Liz and the earl and then told Cecelia, "I've called a cab. It's time you went home, baby."

Cecelia tried not to look too pleased. "All right, Gil," she said gently.

Liz raised an eyebrow. "My, Gil, but you've turned into an autocrat. I wonder Cecelia puts up with such high-handed treatment."

"I'm used to it," Cecelia said sweetly. "My father is Latin American."

Gil grinned. "I've always wanted an obedient wife."

"Well, you've certainly got a dashed lovely one," said Lord Ashbrook with evident admiration. "It's been a pleasure meeting you, Mrs. Archer."

"Thank you, my lord," Cecelia murmured. She smiled at Liz. "It's been a wonderful party, Mrs. Lewis. Thank you so much." Cecelia did not like Liz and had persistently called her Mrs. Lewis all evening, to the barely concealed annoyance of the other woman.

"Liz," she said now for the third time. "After all, Gil and I are quite old friends."

"Really," murmured Cecelia and was dismayed by the pang of jealousy that went through her. Liz Lewis was so elegant and sophisticated; her frosted hair was done so smartly; her conversation was so clever and witty. Gil had spent a good half hour talking to her earlier in the evening after he had drifted away from his wife's little group. Cecelia was afraid he had found their relentlessly horsey conversation extremely boring.

She walked with him now out to the waiting taxi, sleepy and a little let down. No, she did not like Liz Lewis. As the cab pulled away from the hotel Gil said, "I didn't mean to drag you away if you were enjoying yourself. I just thought you had had a long day and must be tired."

"I was very happy to hear you say we were going." She yawned. "I *am* tired."

"My little equestrian." He sounded amused. "And to think I was afraid you wouldn't know anyone at that party."

Her head drooped toward his shoulder and he put an arm around her. Gratefully she nestled against him. "I didn't think I'd know anyone either," she murmured. "Evidently half the Ridgeview Hunt are society big shots. Imagine."

He chuckled and very briefly touched his cheek to her hair. "Imagine," he said. By the time they reached East Seventieth Street she was asleep on his shoulder.

From habit Cecelia awoke very early the following morning. She lay quietly for a minute, her eyes going around the unfamiliar room, remembering last night's party. She sighed a little with pleasure as she realized she did not have to get up and was turning to snuggle back down under the covers when she felt Gil's hand slide over her waist to her hip. Slowly she turned her head on the pillow until she was looking into his eyes.

They seemed startlingly light in his tanned face. "What are you doing awake this early?" she whispered.

"Waiting for you to wake up," he answered. His face looked serious, intent. The underlying amusement it so often held was gone. His hand moved slowly back over her stomach and Cecelia knew he must have felt the flutter of arousal deep in her abdomen. "Cecelia," he said. "You are so sweet." He moved and one hard-muscled leg slid across hers. His lips found the warm valley between her breasts. "I love to make love to you," he murmured.

Cecelia lay perfectly still under his touch. His fingers pushed her nightgown off her shoulders and his lips moved to the breast he had bared. The air conditioning in the apartment was cool but Cecelia felt the heat of his body, the urgent heat of male desire. His hands had moved up under her nightgown.

"Gil," she whispered and her body arched up toward him. The pulse of passion was beginning to pound in her now and her hands went up to hold him. The strong muscles of his back rippled under her touch and he bent to kiss her neck. He caressed her and wooed her with the skill of his hands, the urgency of his kisses. After a few minutes she did not want, could not bear, him to wait any longer. Unbidden, her nails dug into his back. "Gil," she said again, this time more urgently.

"Mmm?" he answered. "Do you need something?" His own voice sounded thicker than usual, but still he held back, teasing her with the caresses of his mouth and hands.

She thought, fleetingly, I wonder which one of

us can hold out the longer? And then, instantly, but I don't want to hold out. She circled his neck with her arms and pulled his head down to hers. "You," she said against his mouth. "I need you."

"Cecelia," he said, "God." His maddening hesitation lasted no longer. With an almost fierce grip he pulled her to him, filling her with the hot pulsing love she wanted so badly.

Cecelia closed her eyes and let him take her to the farthest peaks of passion—the room, the world, everything dropping away from her awareness. All that was left was the feel of Gil and the flooding, shuddering pleasure he gave to her. She struggled briefly to influence their motion, to please *him*, but he was relentless, and at the end, as they shared the transcendent moment of ecstatic union, she knew she would always surrender to him.

Afterward, tangled together, they fell back to sleep again, and Cecelia did not wake until much later in the morning. Gil was once again awake before she was, but this time he was sitting up against the pillows, the blankets pulled over his knees. He had a newspaper propped up and was reading intently.

He did not notice immediately that she was awake and she lay quietly for a moment watching him. His thick fair hair was rumpled and fell across his forehead like an untidy schoolboy's. But the wide, strong shoulders, golden tan against the white sheets, belonged to a man, not a boy. He hadn't shaved yet and his beard glistened like gold thread under his skin.

"Is the world still here?" she asked finally, pushing herself up on her own pillow.

He turned and looked at her, then he put the newspaper down. "Who cares?" he said and reached for her.

Chapter Eight

Cecelia came home from her weekend in New York radiant. They had decided to stay over Sunday night as well, and on Monday morning Gil took a cab to the magazine and Frank came in to drive Cecelia back to Connecticut. It had been a wonderful Sunday, just the two of them, a brief reprise of their honeymoon, and Cecelia hoped that it was a portent of more togetherness for them in the future. It certainly seemed as if Gil were interested in more of a family life.

"We've talked a lot about Jenny," she had said to him over dinner at a small local restaurant Sunday evening, "but we've never talked about having other children. Would you like them?"

"Yes," he had answered instantly. "I want more children." He put down his butter knife and looked at her interrogatively. There was a small frown on his face. "I never thought to ask. Are you on the pill?"

"No," she replied serenely. "I'm not on anything."

The frown lifted and he reached out to touch her hand as it lay on the table holding her wineglass. "My lovely Cecelia," he said softly. "We'll make beautiful children together."

It was wonderful how soft and warm and tender his voice could be. She loved him so much it hurt. "You're certainly trying," she said. He had laughed.

Cecelia solved the problem of someone to do the early barn duty the day that she got home from New York. She and Jennifer had gone over to Hilltop Farm immediately after lunch and discovered that Lady, one of the most valuable school horses, had been lame since Saturday. The mare had come in from the field limping, Marie Rice told Cecelia. "The blacksmith was here, and I had him look at her," she continued. "He couldn't find a thing." Cecelia put in a call to their vet, who said he'd be out later in the afternoon.

Lady had picked up a stone in her foot; it was lodged very deeply. The vet extracted it, and after he had finished Cecelia offered him a cup of coffee. He accepted with alacrity and they both went up to the Vargas house, Cecelia complaining the whole way that she shouldn't have had to call him, that the blacksmith should have found the stone.

Dr. Curran listened to her complain with half an ear; his attention was not on her voice but on her face. She was, he thought painfully, even more beautiful than he remembered.

Tim Curran was twenty-six years old and had been the Hilltop Farm vet for less than a year. He had fallen crashingly in love with Cecelia almost immediately and had been dating her since last

Christmas. He had been going very slowly with her, very carefully, not wanting to make a mistake. He had thought he was making progress when Gilbert Archer had suddenly arrived on the scene. This was the first time Tim had seen her since her marriage and his widely set blue eyes held a hungry look as he watched her fix the coffee.

"So how does it feel to be a married lady?" he asked with a casualness belied by the look in his eyes.

"Very nice," replied Cecelia serenely. She had always tended to regard Tim as a friend rather than a lover and had no idea he had been so badly hurt by her marriage. "Except . . ." she added, a tiny frown indenting her pure brow, "I need to find someone to come in mornings and feed the horses, Tim. Can you think of anyone reliable? Daddy should not be getting up that early and he should not be forking hay."

"Who has been doing it?" he asked, sipping his coffee and watching her over the rim of the cup.

A little color came into her cheeks. "I have. But Gil wants me to find someone else. And he's right. I should be home to see Jenny off to school."

"I see." His voice was expressionless. He took another sip and thought. "There's Harry Amesly," he said finally. "He's always had a horse at his place but the barn burned last week. He's not going to rebuild it, he told me. If you let him stable a horse here, I'm sure he'd do it."

Cecelia smiled at him warmly. "Tim, you're a gem. That would be a perfect solution. I'll talk to him tonight."

"Always glad to be of service," he said, forcing a

lightness he did not feel into his voice. "When is your father coming home?" he asked after a minute's pause.

"Tomorrow."

"Will he be all right living alone here?" Tim took his cup over to the sink. "Has he recovered completely?"

Cecelia sighed. "He says he's great and the doctor says he's doing well but he has to take it easy. The problem is that when it comes to housework and cooking Daddy is a thoroughly Latin American male. He knows what the inside of the kitchen looks like because we eat here, but I doubt if he has ever even boiled water. I'm going to have to get a woman in to take care of him." She smiled wryly at him. "You don't happen to have a cook-housekeeper up your sleeve as well?"

"Sorry." There was a pinched look about his nostrils. "Why can't he stay with you?" he asked bluntly.

"He's going to have to until I find someone," she answered. She stood up. "Thank you for your assistance, doctor," she said with mock solemnity.

He swallowed. "Any time, Cecelia. I'll be in next Monday to give the school horses their shots."

She followed him to the door. "Good. I'll post it on the bulletin board in case any of the owners want to take advantage of your services." She cocked an inquiring eyebrow at him. "School rates?"

He gave a group discount to her when he did the school horses. "If I do it on Monday, tell them they'll get school rates, too," he said.

She grinned. "Plan to be busy." She waved as he went down the path and turned back to the kitchen, heading for the closet where she kept the mops. She couldn't have a housekeeper coming into a dirty house.

Gil did not make it home for dinner that evening. In fact, he didn't make it home at all. A labor problem had arisen, he told Cecelia over the telephone, and he was staying to try to work it out. He would sleep over at the apartment.

She swallowed her disappointment and said, "All right, Gil. I contacted a few agencies today to see about a housekeeper for Daddy, but it's going to take a few days before I can settle on one. Is it all right if he stays here until I can make arrangements?"

"Sure," he said. Then, to someone else, "Tell them I'll be there in a minute." When he came back he sounded preoccupied. "I've got to go, Cecelia. Tell your father to stay for as long as he likes. Frank is going to take you to the airport tomorrow?"

"Yes."

"Good. I'll try to get home tomorrow night, but don't count on me."

"All right," she said evenly. "Good-bye, Gil."

"Good-bye, baby. Give Jen a kiss for me."

"I will," she said. The phone clicked and he was gone.

Ricardo looked wonderful as he got off the plane the following day. He was deeply tanned from the Arizona sun and looked more rested than Cecelia had seen him in years. "You look fantastic," she said as he bent to kiss her. "I can't believe you almost died on me."

"I feel fantastic," he replied. "How are you, *niña*? It is so good to see you again!"

Frank got the baggage in the trunk and Ricardo and Cecelia got in the car's backseat. "Tell me," he said immediately after the door closed behind them, "what has been going on at the farm?"

She laughed. "I've written you *volumes* about everything, Daddy. You know as much as I do."

"How did you do at the Ridge Haven show? I don't know that."

She settled back. "Very well . . ."

In the front seat Frank listened with half an ear to the conversation between father and daughter. For three quarters of the trip it was about horses. The topic changed, however, when Cecelia said, "You're coming to stay with us for a few days, Daddy. You can't go home until we find someone to do your cooking and cleaning. I've got our name in at several agencies; we should find someone soon."

Ricardo frowned. "I would like to go home, Cecelia. I am perfectly fine, I assure you, and I will be more comfortable in my own house."

"Oh, you will, will you?" she retorted. "And what will you eat?"

"I am quite sure I can learn to work the stove," he said stiffly.

"And the washing machine? And vacuum cleaner? And dishwasher?" She was laughing at him.

He smiled a little sheepishly. "You make me sound very useless."

"Totally." She softened her judgment by reaching up and kissing his cheek. "Mrs. Monk did a good job of looking after you the year I was in Colombia, but she's moved to Florida I'm afraid. We'll get someone else soon, but I want you under my eye until we do." Still he hesitated and she added, "Gil wants you to stay too."

Ricardo really had no desire to start learning how to cook and clean at this point in his life. Even in the liberated eighties he was still convinced that housework was a woman's job. He was, as his daughter well knew, a thoroughly Latin American male. He smiled. "All right, *niña*. Until you find someone."

Mrs. Loren, a nice motherly widow, took on the job of housekeeper for Ricardo Vargas, and soon life settled down to what on the surface appeared normality. Ricardo took back his advanced students and left Cecelia the beginners. They split the intermediate riders, Ricardo taking the more serious among them. He also began to coach Cecelia again; it was evident he had his heart set on her winning at the national show in New York in November. Cecelia wanted to win too—and not just for her father.

Cecelia rode and taught during the mornings. In the afternoons she sat around the Archer pool and lifeguarded for Jenny and her friends. The little girl was blossoming, and Cecelia, watching her shouting as she cannonballed off the diving board, would think back to the quiet reserved child she had been and shake her head in wonder. Several afternoons a week Cecelia had adult company at the pool: her father, Marie Rice, one of her college friends, one of the mothers of Jenny's friends. Scarcely ever Gil; he was extremely busy and got home only rarely during the long hot month of July.

Cecelia spent the month waiting for him. When she rode, when she taught, when she played tennis or swam or watched Jenny and her friends, she was outwardly serene but inwardly never at rest. Her whole life was a matter of wondering: When will he come home? When will I see him again? When will we start to live a normal life together? She hated getting into the big lonely bed at night. She did not sleep well when he wasn't there.

All through July she kept thinking that the life they were leading was only temporary, that once the various crises at the office settled down, Gil would have more time for her. It wasn't until he made a two-week trip to England, France, and Germany that she began to realize that perhaps he didn't want to make more time for her, that, unlike her, he was perfectly satisfied with the way things were.

It was to be a working trip, this European jaunt, or so he told her. He had set up a series of appointments with various ministers and bankers and labor leaders. *News Report* was planning an in-depth article on the European economy for the fall. Very hesitantly Cecelia said, "Perhaps I could go with you."

She had been sitting up in bed reading when he came home at ten-thirty. He had kissed her, taken off his jacket and tie, and started to unbutton his shirt. "What did you do today?" he asked. The shirt was off and he stretched as though the muscles in his back were tired.

Cecelia's eyes, watching him, were very dark. "The same old stuff," she had said. "Daddy started Jenny jumping today. She did really well."

"Great." He sat down on a wingback chair and started to take off his shoes.

"Did you get a decent dinner?" she asked quietly.

"Mmm. I ate with Ben and Pat Carruthers, as a matter of fact. And Liz. They were all in the city from Southampton and routed me out of the office."

"Oh," said Cecelia. He went into the bathroom and Cecelia slid down a little on her pillows. This was not the first time by any means that he had dined with friends rather than come home. She felt infinitely forlorn.

He came back into the bedroom, his eyelashes still wet from the washcloth. "By the way," he said, "I'm going abroad for two weeks. I want to get some background for that article I was telling you about. I'll be leaving Tuesday."

That was when she had said, "Perhaps I could go with you."

He looked surprised. "Not this time, baby. I'll take you to Europe, don't worry. But not now."

It was not Europe that she wanted to see. "Why not now?" she persisted. "I won't get in your way, Gil. I promise."

He came over to stand by the bed. "You couldn't ever get in my way," he said tenderly. Cecelia's eyes slid away from his until she was looking once more at her book. Why did his voice have such power over her, she thought painfully. "When I

take you to Europe, I want to have time for you,"
he went on. "Time to show you around myself. I
don't want to have to consign you to American
Express. And Jenny would miss you terribly. We'll
wait until she's back in school."

"All right," she said on a thread of sound. His
hands were on the buckle of his belt, and she put
her book down and slid completely off her pillows
as he finished undressing and got into bed with
her. Yet even as her body automatically responded
to his, a despairing thought flashed across her
mind: this is all he wants from me. During the
daytime it wasn't enough, but for now, as she felt
his mouth touch her cool bare skin, it was.

Gil went off to Europe and the routine of his
home scarcely missed a beat. His wife and daughter continued their daily activities, and one of
them at least was blissfully happy without him.

Cecelia had been right when she thought that
Jenny was blossoming. Cecelia's presence had given
the little girl something she had lacked all her life:
a stable, loving parent who was a steady presence
in her life. She went to Hilltop Farm with Cecelia
every morning; she played at the pool in the afternoon with Cecelia watching; she ate dinner with
Cecelia every night. Cecelia was there to monitor
her television shows, suggest books she might like
to read, crab at her for not keeping her room tidy.
Jenny did not at all mind her father being away;
she liked having her stepmother's undivided attention.

The return home of Ricardo Vargas added another element to Jenny's emotional life that had

been long missing: a doting grandparent. Ricardo's growing attachment to Jenny had surprised Cecelia. He was a man who placed a great deal of importance on blood ties and she wouldn't have thought him capable of so much affection for a child who was unrelated to him.

The fact was that Ricardo missed his daughter, and in his step-granddaughter he had found the perfect solution to fill the gap in his life. The fact that Jennifer obviously thought he was wonderful didn't hurt at all. Soon after his return he took over her lessons himself—a signal honor—and was predicting great things for her future. Cecelia knew he was envisioning Olympic medals, but since Jenny seemed to be thriving on the attention and the work she didn't interfere.

It sometimes seemed to Cecelia that everyone was happy with the arrangements of the Archer-Vargas household except her. Jenny and Ricardo were happy. Gil was happy: he had gotten a mother for his child and a willing partner for his bed. That, apparently, was all he had wanted when he had asked her to marry him. It had become increasingly evident that she was only an adjunct to his life, not an integral part.

It was not a role that satisfied Cecelia. It gave her many material advantages, but material advantages did not interest her. She had not married Gil because he was rich. She had married him because she had thought he was the most wonderful man in the world. He fulfilled all her ideals of what a man ought to be: strong, intelligent, authoritative, good-humored, amusing, kind to those who needed and relied on his strength.

She had loved him when she agreed to marry him, before she knew what it was like to lie in his arms. She loved him now, deeply, achingly, irrevocably. Her whole life had narrowed and the things that once were important to her were important no longer. All that mattered was Gil. If she were with him, if she could rest secure in the knowledge that he loved her as she did him, then she would be happy with the rest of her life. But without that core contentment, all there was for her was restlessness and dissatisfaction. And she was becoming increasingly certain that he did *not* love her—not in the way Cecelia understood love. She was a convenience to him; a convenience he was fond of, but a convenience nonetheless. As beautiful summer day succeeded beautiful summer day and Jenny and Ricardo glowed with health and happiness, Cecelia became increasingly more desolate.

Chapter Nine

Gil came back from his European trip two days earlier than expected. Cecelia was in their bedroom changing for dinner when the door opened and he was there.

"Gil!" she said, surprise in her voice, astonishment on her face. She was standing barefoot in front of the closet wearing a white blouse and blue-flowered skirt; a sandal was in her hand. He started across the room toward her and she dropped the sandal to the floor. Then his arms were around her and her feet were dangling off the floor as he enfolded her in an embrace that left her breathless. "What are you doing home?" she asked when her feet were once more where they should be. "I didn't expect you until the weekend."

"I got everything in I wanted to do, so I decided to catch the next plane home. I got the limousine from the airport."

He looked tired, she thought. "Do you want some dinner? Or is it three in the morning for you? I never can get the time differentials right."

He looked at her crisp skirt and at the jeans that lay carelessly across a chair. "Are you going to eat?"

"Yes. Daddy's coming over."

His silvery eyes remained on her face for perhaps half a minute and then he said, "I could eat something. I want a shower first though."

"Come downstairs when you're ready," she said. "We'll wait. Have you seen Jenny yet?"

"No."

"She'll be thrilled to have you home," said Cecelia with a smile. She slipped her feet into her sandals, tied a ribbon around her pulled-back hair, and walked sedately out of the door.

It didn't seem to Gil as if anyone in his home was thrilled to see him. The biggest welcome he got was from his father-in-law, who had recently read an article about the military government of Chile that he was dying to call to Gil's attention. He talked forcefully about it over a round of cocktails and seemed prepared to continue indefinitely as they sat down to dinner.

"I know, Ricardo, I know," Gil said patiently as he took a bite of his chicken.

"I sometimes wonder if the American attitude toward Latin America comes out of ignorance or arrogance," said Cecelia thoughtfully.

Gil flashed her a quick look. "A bit of both, I expect. And don't forget the profit motive."

Cecelia sighed. "No. One can't ever forget the profit motive."

"Eat your peas, *niña*," said Ricardo.

Startled, Gil looked at his wife's plate.

"I don't *like* peas, Poppy," said Jenny plaintively and Gil finally realized whom Ricardo was addressing.

"We cannot always have what we want in life," Ricardo continued sternly. "They are very good for you." Blue eyes and brown met and held. "Eat half of them," said Poppy.

"Okay." Jenny picked up her fork and heroically took up a portion. "Jessica invited me to go to Riverside with her family next Monday," she said around the mouthful. "Can I go, Cecelia? Please?"

"Do not talk with your mouth full," said Ricardo. "I haven't been to Riverside for years."

Cecelia grinned. "Remember the time you took my Brownie troop?"

He shuddered in mock horror. "Remember? I don't think I shall ever forget." They both broke into laughter.

Gil asked, "What is Riverside?"

Three pairs of eyes swung to his face. "It's an amusement park," his wife told him. "Just over the line in Massachusetts. It's great fun."

"Can I go, then?" Jenny asked. "Jess says they have a flume and a wildcat and a—"

"Yes," Cecelia said hastily. "Yes, Jenny, you can go." A thought belatedly hit her. "That is, if your father approves, of course."

"Certainly she can go if you think it's all right," Gil said quietly.

Jenny washed down her peas with a swallow of milk. "What happened when you took Cecelia's Brownie troop, Poppy?" she asked curiously.

Ricardo proceeded to tell her, helped by some

interpolations from Cecelia. It was a very funny story, at times bordering on hilarious, and Jenny was a bundle of giggles when it concluded. After dessert was served Cecelia told Jenny she could watch one television show and then she was to get into her pajamas. The little girl went obediently upstairs to the room that had been fitted out as a TV-playroom for her, and the three adults went back to the living room.

Gil was very silent, his legs stretched out in front of him as he lounged comfortably on the sofa and listened to his wife and her father. He looked, Cecelia thought, both tired and preoccupied. At nine o'clock Jenny came downstairs again, wearing pink-flowered pajamas. Cecelia got up. "Ready? Say good night then, honey, and we'll go up."

Jenny went over to Ricardo and kissed him. He ruffled her curls and said gently, "Good night, *niña*. Dream about ribbons."

She giggled and went over to where her father was sitting. "Good night, Daddy," she said and kissed him too.

"Good night, sweetheart," he answered. His face looked very grave as Cecelia took his daughter by the hand and walked upstairs with her.

Ricardo rose. "Well, it is time I was going," he said to his son-in-law. "I am happy to see you home again."

Gil had risen as well and now he looked hard into the other man's dark, aquiline face. The brown eyes looking back at him were expressionless. Too expressionless. "Thank you," said Gil. "Good night, Ricardo."

Ricardo did not answer but bowed his head

formally and walked with the ease of familiarity to the door. As he heard it close Gil thoughtfully turned to follow his wife and daughter up the stairs.

Gil did not go into the office the following day. He had run a physically exhausting schedule for the last two weeks and he was tired. When he awoke late in the morning, Cecelia and Jenny had already left for the farm. He had a leisurely breakfast accompanied by the newspaper, and after he had finished he decided to drive over to Hilltop Farm. He had not been there since his marriage.

It looked the same as he drove into the stable yard and parked the BMW next to the Buick station wagon that he had given Cecelia to use. He heard Ricardo's voice coming from the arena and went over to look in the door.

A very large powerful-looking horse was going around the arena ridden by a man whom Gil did not know. The horse was not cooperating and there was evidently a battle of strength in progress. The man was big and strong but the horse was most definitely winning.

"He's all strung out," Ricardo was saying. "Drive him up to the bit. Stop fighting him, George!"

The man cursed as the horse sidled. "He won't straighten out!" he shouted to Ricardo.

"He will if you'll use your legs and stop pulling on his mouth," said Ricardo coldly.

"He's too bloody strong."

Ricardo looked across to the barn doorway. "Cecelia," he called, "will you get on Smokey and show George what I am talking about?"

In a minute his wife came into Gil's field of vision, walking toward the center of the ring. Without a word the rider got off; next to Cecelia he was seen to be a very large man. He easily weighed a hundred pounds more than she did. How in God's name, Gil thought distractedly, did Ricardo think one hundred and ten pounds could do what two hundred and ten could not? The horse looked to be a brute.

Cecelia swung into the saddle, shortened the stirrups, and began to walk the horse around the ring. After a minute she moved into a trot and as Gil watched, astonished, the one hundred and ten pounds began to do what the two hundred and ten could not. The horse's hind legs were driven up under him and his whole way of moving changed. In ten minutes she had him cantering, collected and sweet as butter, going smoothly around the ring.

"All right," Ricardo called and she brought the horse down to a walk, patted him and fussed over him, then walked him back to his owner. "That is what I was talking about," Ricardo said pleasantly. "Riding has nothing to do with physical strength. Anyone, no matter how strong, who gets into a pulling contest with a horse is going to lose."

"Yeah," said George. "I see what you mean."

Cecelia handed him back his reins and her eyes, moving past her father, caught sight of her husband in the doorway. "Gil!" she said, astonished. "Whatever are you doing here?" She came across the ring toward him, and as she drew closer he could see the sweat on her forehead and nose. Her yellow shirt was damp.

"What are *you* doing here in this heat?" he returned.

"Jenny and I just came over for a short while," she answered, wiping her forehead with the back of her arm. "It *is* hot."

"Cecelia!" a little girl called from the barn. "Telephone! It's Dr. Curran."

"Oh, good," said Cecelia. "I'll be right back," she flung at her husband as she dashed toward the barn. Gil stayed where he was, watching the man called George trying to emulate Cecelia's success with his horse. Ricardo's instructions were clear, succinct, and merciless. When Cecelia came back from the barn she went over to talk to him for a minute and then returned to Gil's side. "How about going home for a swim?" she asked. "Or are you going into the office today?"

"No." He did not smile. "No, I'm taking the day off."

"I'm glad to hear that," she said, brown eyes reflecting concern. "You were awfully tired last night. You still look tired."

"Is this a complaint?" he asked softly. He had not been too tired to make passionate love to her last night.

The beautiful color rose in her cheeks. "No, it is not a complaint. As you well know."

They stared at each other in silence and then another voice called, "Cecelia!"

With an effort Cecelia looked away from him. "What is it, Jenny?"

"Can Jess and Meredith come swim at my pool this afternoon?"

"Yes—if they ask their mothers first."

"They already did," Jenny said blithely and Gil laughed.

"She's got your number, baby."

Cecelia sighed. "Isn't it disgusting?"

They sat around the pool all afternoon, diving in whenever it got too hot in the sun. Gil spent a half hour tossing his daughter and her friends up in the air, which they loved if their giggles and shrieks were anything to go by. Cecelia smiled with pleasure watching him. Gil was so good with children, she thought. If only he were home more . . .

"Did I once complain that Jen was too quiet?" he asked his wife as he came over and sat down on the chaise longue next to hers. "I must have been mad." The three girls were playing a water game on their own now and the whole yard reverberated to the cries of "Marco!" "Polo!"

Cecelia chuckled. "She's changed."

"So I notice," and he winced exaggeratedly as Jenny emitted a particularly shrill shriek. He picked up a towel and rubbed the water out of his hair, then lay back and closed his eyes. Cecelia closed hers as well. It was such a simple thing, she thought, to make her so happy: sitting by the pool with her husband while their daughter played with her friends.

"I'm roasting," Cecelia said after ten minutes. Gil opened his eyes and watched as she walked out onto the diving board and stood poised there for a minute while she waited for the girls to clear out of her way. She was wearing a faded turquoise racing suit that hugged the lines of her lithe young body. He had missed that body while he was in

Europe. Badly. Badly enough, in fact, to cram four days of appointments into two and come home early.

At four-thirty Cecelia called, "All right, girls. Start to get your things together and I'll drive you home."

Gil's hand reached over and covered her. "Frank's here. He can drive them."

"I don't mind. I know where they both live."

"*I* mind," he replied, his eyes becoming very smoky. "I have other predinner plans for you."

His fingers were on her wrist and she knew he must feel the sudden acceleration of her pulse. "Do you, my lord?" she asked with faint irony.

He stood up, her hand still in his. As she rose to stand next to him he remarked, "If I remember correctly, I once told someone I'd always wanted an obedient wife."

She managed to look faintly affronted. "I stand before you, master, humble and awaiting your pleasure."

"Not here!" he replied in horror. "Think of the children."

Her mouth quivered but she preserved her gravity. "I don't know," she said with thought. "It would be so educational. They take sex ed in school, after all."

He frowned and then said consideringly, "Perhaps you're right." He put his hand on the strap of her suit as if to pull it down and she squeaked and jumped away from him. He grinned. "No more back chat, wife. Get moving."

"You think you're so smart." But she was smiling as well and moved with no reluctance at all toward the house. Late that afternoon, in the cool privacy of their air-conditioned bedroom, he got her with child.

The following day Gil went back to work. He called The Birches at four o'clock only to hear from Nora that his wife was not at home. He called the Vargas house and got no answer. Next he tried the barn. "Hilltop Farm," a familiar voice said.

"Is that you, Jen?"

"Oh, hi, Daddy. Yeah, it's me. What do you want?"

"Is Cecelia around?"

"Just a minute." For perhaps three minutes Gil waited on the line; it was not an experience he was accustomed to. "Daddy? Cecelia's busy just now. Dr. Curran is here. She says can I take a message or do you want her to call you back?"

Gil frowned. "No," he said then. "She doesn't have to call me back. I'll see you at dinner."

"Oh, are you coming home for dinner?" His daughter's voice held only innocent surprise.

"Yes," he said.

"I'll tell Cecelia. Bye Daddy."

"Good-bye."

Gil hung up the phone and remained staring at it for a minute. There was a knock on the door of his office and his assistant editor came in. "Do you want to go over that material?" he asked his boss.

Gil stood up. "I want *you* to go over it, Hank. You know what we're looking for. You've been doing this magazine for as long as I have."

Hank Barber did know what to do, but he had

never been allowed to operate without the boss's keen eye looking over his shoulder. "Will you want to see it in the morning?" he asked.

Gil looked at him. "No. This is an area of the operation I am getting out of. As of today, Hank, you are in charge. If I don't like what you're doing"—he grinned—"I'll fire you."

After an astonished pause Hank grinned back. "You won't have to fire me, Gil."

"I know that. I should have turned this over to you years ago. I don't have to have my finger on every piece of the pie."

"You did, at the beginning. But you've trained us all pretty well over the years."

Gil raised an eyebrow. "I'm not retiring, Hank."

His subordinate laughed with genuine amusement. "I don't think you ever will."

Gil went over to the closet for his suit jacket. He had planned to stay at the magazine until much later and so had not told Frank to come in to get him. "Does anyone around here have a train schedule to Connecticut?" he asked Hank.

His wife was a little abstracted during dinner and the reason for it came out after Jennifer went upstairs. Cecelia had had a telephone call from Pat Carruthers, inviting them to Southampton for the weekend. "She's having a house party and wants to know if we can come. She apologized for the lateness of the invitation but she thought you'd still be in Europe. I said I'd get back to her. Senator Bayley will be there."

"Oh, good," said Gil. "Call her back, baby, and say we'll come."

"All right," said Cecelia slowly.

"What's the matter? Don't you want to go?" They were having coffee in the living room and he put down his cup and looked at her, a puzzled expression on his face.

As a matter of fact she didn't. She was sure Liz Lewis would be there. But all she said was, "Nora and Frank go on vacation this Saturday. I suppose Jenny can always go to stay with Daddy for the weekend."

"I'm sure they'd both love it," he said promptly.

"Yes."

"Is there something else?"

She forced a smile. "No. Baron's foot was operated on this afternoon and I guess I'm just a little worried about him. But Tim says he thinks he'll be okay, and Daddy will be around to change the bandages all weekend."

His face was very still. "Tim? Who is Tim?"

"Tim Curran," she answered. "Dr. Curran. Our vet."

"Oh," said Gil quietly. Then, "I see."

"Cecelia!" said Jenny, coming into the room. "I'm ready. Come on up with me."

Cecelia rose. "Kiss your father good night."

Gil kissed Jennifer and tickled her and made her giggle. But as Cecelia led her out of the room his eyes were not on his daughter but on the slim figure of his wife. He looked like a man who had just received some very unpleasant news.

Chapter Ten

Ricardo was delighted to take Jenny for the weekend, and so late on Friday morning Gil and Cecelia got in the BMW and headed for Long Island. Cecelia had never before been across the Throgs Neck Bridge. Gil was astounded. "Haven't you ever been to the ocean?"

"Of course. Don't be so superior. Rhode Island is on the ocean. So is the Cape."

He smiled a little, his hands steady on the wheel, his eyes on the highway. "The only person more insular than a New Englander is a New Yorker. Sorry."

There was a pause and then she said with a studied casualness, "Who else is likely to be there, do you know?"

"I haven't the foggiest," he answered cheerfully, "but it should be a good mix. Pat knows how to entertain."

And she didn't. He didn't say that but Cecelia read it between the lines. He never suggested inviting anyone to The Birches. She felt sunk in gloom.

The Carruthers' waterfront home was magnifi-

cent—larger even than The Birches. Gil pulled
the car up to the awninged carport and a servant
came out to take their cases. As they stepped into
the hall Pat came through from another room.
"Gil, darling," she said and kissed him. "How lovely
to see you. And Cecelia."

Cecelia held out her hand. She had her father's
reserve about kissing strangers. "Thank you," she
said. "Pat."

"Come along out to the porch," Pat said gaily.
"Have you had lunch?"

"Yes." Gil put a hand on Cecelia's bare arm; she
was wearing a sleeveless cotton dress. "We stopped
on the way out."

The first person Cecelia saw when they reached
the porch was Liz Lewis. She was wearing white
tennis shorts and looked tanned and marvelous.
"Gil!" she called. "Come and tell me about your
descent on Europe."

Cecelia foresaw that it was going to be a very
long weekend.

In fact, Cecelia thought as she sat on the beautiful beach late the following afternoon, it would
have been a weekend to enjoy if she had felt more
at ease about Gil. The guests had proved to be
interesting and surprisingly easy and pleasant; she
had never found herself in the embarrassing isolation that had occurred briefly at Liz's New York
party. On the contrary, she never seemed to get a
minute by herself.

Gil looked to be having a marvelous time. If she
were surrounded he was no less so. She could
understand why. Quite simply, he was more fun

than anyone else there. He was witty, knowledgeable, amusingly opinionated, and he had a fund of good stories that were endlessly entertaining. No wonder, she thought, all these bright, intelligent people crowded around him. Probably they were being so nice to her because she was his wife.

Two people, at any rate, were pleased to see her for herself. Maisie Winter was there with her husband Hal. And the Carruthers' neighbors, who came over for dinner, brought with them a young French novelist who was staying with them for the weekend. He was about twenty-seven and good-looking in a dark, intensely serious fashion. He had a slight problem in fitting in with the rest of the party: he spoke no English and no one had read his book.

Cecelia's kind heart was wrung, and after dinner she approached him and said in soft, fluent French, "I must tell you how extraordinary I found your book, Monsieur Peyre."

The intense dark eyes lit up and he broke into rapid speech—almost the first words he had uttered since arriving. Cecelia replied, and that was it for the evening. He hung on to her with grim determination, the dark eyes clearly showing it was not just her French he appreciated.

After dinner they had moved out onto the Carrutherses' enormous screened-in porch. Maisie Winter sat a little apart from the rest of the group and watched Gilbert Archer and his wife. Gil was standing, drink in hand, by one of the screened windows. He was listening gravely to Senator Bayley, and as the senator finished, Gil's mouth quirked. He said something that caused both the senator and Liz Lewis, who was standing by Gil's side, to break into laughter. Pat had lit a few hurricane lamps and one of them was next to Gil; the flickering light from it rimmed his fair hair with silver. His face was brilliant with intelligence and mirth. Slowly Maisie looked from it to his wife.

Cecelia was seated in a wicker chair, and next to her, on a wicker stool, was Marc Peyre, the young French novelist. He was talking. As Maisie watched, Cecelia's eyes slowly traveled to the figure of her husband across the width of the porch from her. There was a wistful, uncertain look about her mouth.

Damn, said Maisie to herself. Damn, damn, damn.

"What's the matter, dear?" said her husband, coming up and sitting beside her.

"I'm worried about Cecelia," she answered.

"Cecelia?" He sounded startled. "Why? She's a lovely girl. Getting along just fine."

"I know she's a lovely girl," his wife answered impatiently. "I've known her since she was a child. She has something rare in this day and age, Hal; she's generous and she's kind. Look at her boring herself into a coma over that boy and his wretched book. And all because she feels sorry for him."

"How do you know it's a wretched book?" her husband asked reasonably. "You haven't read it."

"It must be," said Maisie. She was not interested in the book. "I don't know how she came to marry Gil Archer," she went on, "but I'm sure it was a mistake. She's not in his class at all."

"What do you mean?" Her husband sounded

genuinely puzzled. "Any woman would have jumped at the chance to marry Gil."

"That's just it," his wife said infuriatingly.

"Could you possibly be a little less sibylline?" he asked patiently.

"Gil is spoiled rotten," she said with admirable clarity. "All his life he's gotten just what he wanted. Even when he went against his father and started the magazine, he had it easy. He didn't need his father's backing. He had all the Van Gelder money from his mother's legacy to stake him."

"I thought you liked Gil," said Hal.

"I do. I defy you to find me a woman who doesn't. And that is just the trouble. He has only to smile that bone-melting, charming smile, to give that look of secret amusement, and they fall into his lap like ripe plums. A man like that is no good for Cecelia. She's too vulnerable, too young for his kind of sophistication. It will only lead to heartache."

"But I haven't heard that he's been unfaithful," protested Hal.

His wife gave him a pitying look. "There's more to marriage than sexual fidelity," she said. "Let's go and rescue Cecelia from the French."

Cecelia, like Hal, had not heard of Gil's being unfaithful. It was not unfaithfulness that she feared. She satisfied him in that respect; she knew that. But a real marriage, as Maisie had recently pointed out, was more than just being good in bed together. With an aching heart, she was coming to see that she did not have a real marriage at all.

There was nothing she could do about it, nothing she could say to him. She was intensely conscious of being under an obligation to him about her father's hospital bills. All the benefits from their marriage were on her side—how then could she complain?

She and Gil played tennis the following day, a mixed doubles match against Liz Lewis and Ben Carruthers. As Cecelia watched Liz toss the ball high in the air and serve to Gil she thought dismally that if Liz had been a more motherly type Gil would probably have married *her*. Liz's serve was hard and deep and Gil returned it with an equally hard forehand.

Cecelia was not at all happy about playing in such expert company. The superb coordination and timing that made her such an excellent rider enabled her to pick up most sports easily, but better than average was not good enough here. She had played tennis in high school and college, though not seriously, and after two points she knew she was hopelessly outclassed.

Gil, on the other hand, she knew for an excellent player, and she shamelessly stepped aside and let him take as many chances as he could. He was strong enough to cover her defects and the score held even. As the game went along she began to relax a little; her husband was laughingly encouraging; obviously he was playing for fun, not blood. Cecelia ventured to become a little more aggressive and he called approval as she tackled a difficult backhand and returned it to the opposite corner for a winner. "That's my girl," he said as he passed her on the way to the net and she felt absurdly pleased. Her eyes began to sparkle. She was actually beginning to have fun.

Fifteen minutes later the score was 4–5 and Gil was serving for the set. Cecelia stood at the net, her racquet poised to volley. Gil's serve cannon-balled over the net and Ben flung out his racquet and managed a crosscourt return. Cecelia got it and volleyed into the court directly in front of her. Liz, seeing it coming, had already prepared. She took the ball on her racquet and then slammed it hard, directly at Cecelia's face.

Cecelia's excellent reflexes saved her. She didn't get her racquet up but she ducked, and the ball grazed the top of her head as it went by. "Sorry, Cecelia," said Liz sweetly, "but you shouldn't be so close to the net."

Cecelia was very pale. "Come on back to the baseline, baby," said Gil. She backed up slowly, her eyes on the ground at her feet. "Are you all right?" he asked. His voice sounded peculiar.

"Yes," she said without looking at him. "I'm okay."

Gil picked up the tennis balls. "Love–fifteen," he said. Liz, in the ad court waiting to receive serve, smiled. Gil had a tremendously powerful serve. Ben had had trouble with it all morning, but Gil always took something off it when he served to a woman. Liz had made most of her team's points. Gil threw the ball high in the air and his arm came around. The ball was by Liz before she even got her racquet back. "I believe that was in," he called to Ben.

"It was. An ace." Ben was not smiling as he moved back to the baseline.

"Fifteen—all," said Gil as he picked up the ball Ben had thrown to him. He walked toward Cecelia. "Stay at the baseline, baby," he told her. "We'll finish this game in a hurry."

He was right. Ben managed to get a racquet on his serve but lost the point. Gil aced Liz once more and Ben ended it by hitting Gil's first serve into the net.

Ben came immediately to the net to shake Gil's hand. "I don't blame you," was what he said. Then he grinned at Cecelia. "You have the makings of a wicked backhand there, Cecelia. Get this guy to coach you a little."

Both men walked with Cecelia to the umbrella table beside the court, where they joined the group who had been watching the match. Neither Ben nor Gil said a word to Liz.

"That was stupid," Pat Carruthers said to Liz a little later in the privacy of the house.

"I know." Liz did not look happy. "I did it before I thought."

"Ben is furious with you. He likes Cecelia. He says she's what Gil's needed for a long time."

"Thanks," said Liz acidly.

"I didn't say it," Pat protested. "Ben did."

"She's very beautiful," Liz conceded.

"She is. Intelligent too. Speaks beautiful French— thank God. What I was going to do with that novelist I don't know. His book is evidently one of those avant-garde things the French intelligentsia read and no one else. Melissa said he arrived armed with an introduction from Pierre Desmoulin and they had to entertain him for the weekend.

She apologized most profusely for saddling me with him last night."

"Cecelia had read his book," said Liz.

"She probably had to read it in college."

"Do me a favor, Pat," said Liz. "Don't try to cheer me up. It depresses the hell out of me."

Liz apologized to Cecelia before dinner that evening, and Cecelia, surprised and touched by her obvious humility, was very gracious. "Don't worry about it," she said with a smile.

"I don't know what got into me," Liz said.

"The competitive spirit, I expect," returned Cecelia. "When one plays as well as you do, one doesn't like to lose."

"You're probably right," Liz said slowly, her eyes steady on the lovely face of Gil's wife. "I don't like to lose." She saw a familiar figure in the corner of her vision and turned to call, "Gil, darling, I've just apologized to Cecelia for my tennis excesses and she has said I'm forgiven. Will you forgive me as well?"

Cecelia turned also and both women watched the tall male figure approaching them. He was wearing casual white pants, a light blue golf shirt, and top-siders.

"Certainly," he said as he came up to them. He looked quizzically at Liz. "As long as it doesn't happen again," he added.

"I've learned my lesson," said Cecelia comically. "Next time I won't hang over the net."

Gil looked at her. "Your unconquerably sweet disposition is a constant amazement to me, baby."

Cecelia flushed a little and Liz's mouth tightened.

"Is Monsieur Peyre returning tonight?" she asked sweetly.

"I hope not," said Gil. "As the only person here who's read his bloody book, poor Cecelia is the one who gets stuck." He frowned a little. "How *did* you come to read it, anyway?" he asked.

"I read it for a French lit course in college." She grinned. "It's definitely the sort of book you only come across in lit courses."

"Was it any good?" asked Liz curiously.

"It was very clever," Cecelia temporized.

"Was it interesting?" asked Gil.

Cecelia made a face. "Monumentally dull. All form and no subject, if you know what I mean."

"Yes," said Gil ruefully. "I do." He looked around the lawn which was empty now of people. "I think it's time we changed for dinner."

The dinner party on Sunday night was considerably smaller than Saturday's had been. A number of guests had departed after lunch, but Gil, who hated driving in traffic, planned to stay until Monday. M. Peyre did not come back and Cecelia had a pleasant dinner conversation with Maxwell Withers, president of Westchester's largest bank. Mr. Withers appeared to derive a good deal of pleasure from their talk and showed every sign of wanting to continue it after dinner ended and they removed to the porch. They were joined shortly by the president of one of the top Fortune 500 companies and then a few other men and women. The conversation became general and Cecelia sat back a little, no longer contributing but listening gravely. All these people were intelligent, moderate, tolerant, and well informed. The world they inhabited seemed a different place from the world reflected in the news headlines she read.

Perhaps she too would be like this, she thought, if her life hadn't been touched by the tragedy of Argentina. But because of what had happened to her cousins, to boys who had visited Connecticut often in her childhood, who had mended her dolls and taught her to climb trees, she could never rest secure that the world was a safe, sane, and just place. There was terror out there, and pain, and hunger and injustice. One may not be able to do very much about it, she thought, but at least one should be *aware*.

Gil was not part of her group, and she looked for him and found him standing with Ben Carruthers in the corner of the porch. They were deep in conversation. As Cecelia watched, Ben took out a pack of cigarettes and offered one to Gil. Her husband shook his head in refusal, and Ben lit one for himself and put the pack away. Cecelia reflected that she hadn't seen Gil with a cigarette since they had married. She remembered Dr. Stein's admonition to him that if her father had been a smoker he would have been dead. Gil had evidently taken those words to heart. Cecelia was grateful; she might not be completely happy with her marriage but she had no desire at all to find herself a wealthy widow.

Ben commented on Gil's abstinence as well. "Have you given up smoking? After all these years?"

"I have," Gil replied pleasantly. "When I married Cecelia I just stopped. It wasn't as bad as I thought it would be."

"Oho," said Ben. "Cecelia was after you about it?"

"She never said a word." Gil picked up his drink from the table. "But she doesn't like it. So I quit." He arched an eyebrow. "Don't blow your polluted smoke in my face, please."

Ben laughed. "There's nothing worse than a reformed smoker."

"So they say." Gil looked at his empty glass. "I haven't reformed my drinking, though," he said pointedly.

"The bar is inside," said Ben. "Go get it yourself."

"Is that any way to treat a guest?" demanded Gil.

"You're not a guest. You're a friend."

"Is that supposed to be a compliment?" Gil asked. Ben watched as he made his way across the porch, stopping by his wife's side as he passed her. After a minute she detached herself from her group and accompanied him inside the house.

"Were you enjoying your conversation?" Gil asked her blandly as he waited for the barman to pour his drink. She looked at him doubtfully. "You can tell me, baby. I won't give you away."

"Well, they're all very nice people, of course."

"Cecelia," he said rebukingly. "You can do better than that."

"They *are* nice," she repeated. "Polite, urbane, sane, careful."

"They are." Gil handed her a glass of white wine. "Isn't it suffocating?"

She looked at him thoughtfully. "It's never-never land. It would be nice if the world were like Mr.

Withers envisions it, but it isn't. Doesn't he ever read the newspapers?"

"Only the financial page, I expect." He took his own drink and leaned back against the wall, regarding her out of inscrutable eyes. "My father was just like them. That's why I didn't go into banking."

"I see," said Cecelia.

"Yes." Gil's voice was slow and considering. "Yes. I believe you do."

Chapter Eleven

The drive home Monday morning seemed to fly by. They talked. They talked as they had never talked before. Cecelia told him about her cousins, about the terrible letter from her Uncle Fernando that had brought the news of their disappearance.

"That was three years ago," she said somberly. "Since then we have heard nothing of their whereabouts."

"About eight to ten thousand people share their fate," Gil said. "I don't know if you're ever going to find out what happened to them, Cecelia. The military leaders in Argentina are afraid that if the fates of those who disappeared are revealed the relatives will insist on the punishment of those involved."

"The government was involved," Cecelia said bitterly.

"Of course it was. But it won't admit that."

"It's so terrible, Gil. And what's even more terrible is to hear men like Maxwell Withers talking so dispassionately about the 'risks' of financial transactions with Latin America. They *like* the military dictatorships. They're more stable, they say."

"Well they are," returned Gil calmly. "They beat the country into submission and American commerce can operate without fear of losing its investment."

"It's immoral," she said stubbornly.

"Not to Maxwell Withers. Nor was it immoral to my father. The Knickerbocker Bank, of which he was the president for many years, made a great number of loans to Latin American dictatorships."

"I see," said Cecelia.

There was about five minutes of silence as Gil drove through the tollgate on the Throgs Neck Bridge and got into the right lane for the New England Thruway. Once they were on the correct road he allowed his attention to relax a fraction. "We might do an article on Argentina," he said. "I don't think it would produce any names for you, but it would make a few people very uncomfortable."

"That would be worth something," she said tightly.

"Yes, it would." He grinned crookedly. "That's why I started the magazine, after all. To stir things up, to reveal what the bureaucrats didn't want revealed." His voice was calm and emotionless but Cecelia had learned to read him, a little.

"You have a passion for justice, don't you, darling?" she said softly.

He sent her a swift sidelong look. "You're the first person to find me out," he said with a strange note in his voice.

"I have been reading your magazine very carefully for quite a few months now," she said. A small smile touched the corners of his mouth, but his eyes did not turn from the road. They finished the last fifteen minutes of the drive in comfortable silence.

It was a lovely homecoming. Jenny was happy to have them back, and the whole family—including Ricardo—spent a lazy contented afternoon around the swimming pool. The following day, when Gil went off to work and she and Jenny prepared to go over to the farm, Cecelia felt happier than she had in many weeks. Something important had happened between her and Gil this past weekend; she felt it, felt that their relationship had moved onto a new level. She began to be hopeful about the future.

Gil too was regarding his marriage with new eyes. The reassessment had begun in Europe, actually, where he had found himself missing Cecelia most damnably. It was then he had decided to try to rearrange his schedule so he could spend more time with her. She had wanted to come with him and he should have brought her. It simply hadn't occurred to him to do so at the time. Now he decided it was time he grew accustomed to the fact that he had a wife.

The Rosses were on vacation for two weeks so Gil was driving himself. At three-thirty he decided he had done enough for the day and left for home. There was no one at The Birches when he arrived so he changed his clothes and headed for the one place he was sure his wife and daughter would be.

The Buick wagon was parked in the stable yard,

and Jennifer was in the tack room with several other little girls. "Hi, Daddy," she greeted him. "Cecelia's up at the house." He could hear their giggles as he headed toward the path, and he smiled.

The smile left his face as soon as he opened the kitchen door. A strange young man was there, naked to the waist, and beside him stood Gil's wife. She was looking up at the stranger and laughing.

It was only a second before they turned to see Gil in the door, but the twosome before him seemed frozen, as in a still frame, in the camera of his brain: the man's body, the flat stomach and narrow hips, the bared torso tanned a deep Indian brown, Cecelia's laughing face, her slender hand lying caressingly on the muscled upper arm. "Gil!" said Cecelia. "I didn't expect to see you so early."

"There wasn't anyone home so I came over here." His voice was quiet, ominously so.

"Dr. Curran came this afternoon to check Baron. I'm afraid Baron bit him for his trouble," she explained. "I've just been administering first aid." For the first time Gil noticed the bandage on the muscled upper arm of the young vet. "I don't think you've ever met Dr. Curran," his wife was going on. "Tim, this is my husband."

Gil looked into a pair of wide-set blue eyes that held his with obstinate directness. "How do you do," said Tim Curran.

Gil nodded. "Dr. Curran." Neither man made any attempt to shake the other's hand.

Cecelia turned her attention back to the vet.

"Tim, I'm most terribly sorry about this. He's usually such a sweet-tempered pony."

"Don't worry, Cecelia." The young doctor picked his shirt up from the kitchen chair and proceeded to put it on. "He's looking fine. You can start to work him a little—just walk and trot for a week."

"Okay." She smiled up at him, her emotions clear on her face. "You did a super job, Tim. I would have hated to lose that pony."

He smiled back, and Gil had no difficulty in recognizing the emotion in the dark blue eyes. "I'm here whenever you need me," Tim Curran said. And looked at Cecelia's husband.

Gil stared back, his own eyes so pale and cold they looked like pieces of glass. "Good-bye, Dr. Curran," he said.

Cecelia frowned, a little disturbed by the abruptness of his tone. She felt terrible about Tim's being bitten. "I'll walk with you to your car," she said. She sent her husband a brief smile. "I'll be right back."

She stayed a few minutes at the door of Tim's car, chatting, and then stepped back, waved, and turned to retrace her steps. She saw Gil by the tack room and moved to join him. "We can go home now, if you like," she said.

"Fine." His voice sounded peculiar—the same way it had sounded on the tennis court after Liz had slammed that ball at her. She realized with a little dismay that he was angry. Something must have happened at the office.

"I'll take Jenny in the wagon," she offered. He nodded briefly and strode to where he had parked the BMW. Cecelia watched as he pulled out of the stable yard, a small frown between her brows. Then she called to Jenny and the two of them got into the station wagon to follow Gil home.

Since Nora was on vacation, Cecelia sent Jenny upstairs to work on a summer book report and she began to prepare dinner herself. Gil went into the library, and when she looked in to see if he wanted a drink it was to find he had already made a start. The scotch in his glass was almost finished. At her appearance he got up and went over to the liquor cart and began to make himself another. "Can I fix you something?" he asked.

"No. I have to finish doing the dinner. I just thought I'd tell you to go ahead without me."

"I already have, as you see." His voice was pleasant.

"Yes." Cecelia backed to the door. "Dinner will be ready in about an hour."

He had time for three more scotches before dinner. He usually had a glass of wine with his meal but tonight he had several. He seemed perfectly all right to Cecelia's apprehensive eyes, only very silent.

Jenny didn't appear to notice any change in her father and chattered away unself-consciously. Cecelia tried once or twice to draw Gil into the conversation; she had no success. He had come home early from work looking for her—the first time he had ever done so—and she had not been there. She thought he was annoyed at her for spending so much time over at the farm. "I don't usually go over to the farm in the afternoons," she offered as she collected the dishes to bring them to the kitchen. "It was just because of Tim that I went today."

There was a distinctly nasty curve to his mouth. "So I gathered," he said, and Cecelia felt her cheeks begin to burn. She had never heard him use that tone of voice.

She was extremely reluctant to go upstairs to her bedroom that night. After dinner Gil had had several more drinks and his quiet brooding presence began to take on the aura of a threat. It came to Cecelia, as she slowly climbed the stairs with him at eleven-thirty, that she was afraid.

It was a shock. She had never in her life been afraid of a man. Her father had always adored his little equestrian. Her husband had always been infinitely gentle with her, infinitely tender. And now she stood in her bedroom with him and the physical threat of his presence seemed to vibrate through the room. Why was he so angry?

"Did something happen at the office today?" she ventured as he closed the door with unnecessary force.

He smiled and she felt her throat close with fear. "No," he said softly. "Not at the office." He crossed the few feet of floor that separated them and took hold of her. His fingers were hard and bruising on the soft bare flesh of her upper arms. His strength had always been something she rejoiced in; never had it been exerted against her, as it was now. He kissed her.

There was no tenderness in his mouth or his hands, no love. Instead there was anger and punishment and—most frightening of all—raw passion. He had never before demanded a response from

her; always before he had asked. Cecelia was motionless in his hold, swept by a tide of fear and
violent physical sensation.

When he raised his head at last she remained
perfectly still. Some instinct told her that resis-
tance from her was what he wanted—he wanted a
fight to stoke his anger. So she didn't move but
kept still and frozen as a statue; the only motion
about her was the slow trickle of blood that dripped
from a cut on her lip. "I'm sorry, Gil," she breathed.
"I don't know what I've done to make you so
angry, but I'm sorry."

He stared, fascinated, at the blood on her lip.
He noticed with a corner of his brain that she was
trembling. He looked into her eyes and saw she
was afraid of him. "I'm sorry," she whispered,
and all at once he was appalled at what he was
doing. Cecelia had been right; he had wanted a
fight. He looked now at his wife, at the eyes of a
frightened child that looked back at him; he heard
again the bewildered pleading tones of her voice,
and he was suddenly sick at the thought of what
he had done to reduce her to this.

He dropped his hands and stepped back. "God,
Cecelia," he said. "I'm sorry."

She seemed to have ceased breathing, but at his
words a deep shudder went through her. She wet
her lips with her tongue and tasted the salt of her
own blood. "But what is the matter?" she whispered.

He dropped heavily into the nearest chair, and
elbows on his knees, he raised his hands to his
face. Cecelia stared at him, stared at the fists that
were clenched to his forehead. His knuckles were
white with pressure. He knew what he was suffer-

ing from and he didn't like it one bit: temper and wounded vanity. Because of that he had tried to hurt Cecelia. God, he thought. What's gotten into me?

"Gil?" She was kneeling in front of him now. She put her hands on his to remove them from his face. As she slid her fingers along to his wrists she could feel the thundering of his pulse. "Gil," she repeated, "darling."

He left his hands in hers and looked at the face that was uplifted to his. She had never seemed more beautiful. He tried, desperately, to get a grip on himself. He couldn't touch her now. He was afraid of himself, afraid of the violence he still felt within. "I'm sorry," he repeated. "I don't know what made me take my bad temper out on you. I drank too much." His level voice was belied by the hammering pulse in his wrists. Gently, he removed his hands from hers. Slowly she stood up and he followed her. "Go to bed," he said. "I'm going down to the kitchen to make myself a pot of coffee."

"Do you want me to make it for you?" she asked.

"No!" He managed a smile. "No. Allow me the dignity of sobering up in solitude."

With somber eyes she watched him walk to the door. His steps were perfectly even. As she undressed for bed she discovered that her hands were still shaking.

He left for New York early the following morning and didn't return until late at night. It was a pattern he repeated all week. The only way he could think of to resolve his own emotional turmoil was to keep as far away from his wife as possible.

Cecelia, for her part, never reproached him for his absences, never asked where he had been. But then, he thought with weary bitterness, she had never complained about his neglect. If he had wanted a wife who was the direct opposite of Barbara he had gotten her. The supreme irony was that he would have welcomed a show of possessiveness from Cecelia.

The image of his wife and Tim Curran, linked together in intimate association, haunted him. Tim, he remembered, was the fellow who could see her "anytime." Tim was the fellow she had been dating before she met him, before he rescued her father and blackmailed her into marrying him. Tim was the fellow for whose telephone calls she jumped, for whose visits she waited.

Gil stayed away from home as much as he could, and when he did put in an appearance Cecelia usually only saw him in bed. He never again made love to her in anger. But all the extreme tenderness that had characterized his lovemaking in the past was gone. Passion remained, flaming and intense, but the sweetness that had melted her heart had vanished.

At the end of September Cecelia paid a visit to the gynecologist and had her suspicions confirmed. She was pregnant. Gil was sleeping over in the New York apartment that week and she didn't have an opportunity to tell him until Friday night. She was sitting up in bed reading when he came in at eleven. She closed her book and put it on the bedside table. He was loosening his tie.

"How are things going?" she asked. She might have been addressing a casual acquaintance at a cocktail party.

"All right. The article on Argentina is looking good." His tie was off and he dropped it on a chair and began to unbutton his shirt. "How have you been?"

She bent her head and looked at the mound her drawn up knees made under the covers. "Fine," she said. "You might be interested to know that I'm pregnant."

His hand fell from his shirt button. "What?" He swung around to stare at her.

She kept her head down. "That's right. I went in to see Dr. Harknis today. She says the baby's due in May."

"Cecelia," he said. His only view was the shining brown crown of her head. "Cecelia." He walked over to the bed and sat down. He didn't know what to say.

Finally she raised her head. Her eyes were dark and unreadable. "Are you happy?" she asked.

"Of course I'm happy. Are you?"

"I suppose so. I asked the doctor if I could ride in the National in November and she said I could. Will that be all right with you?"

A muscle flickered in his jaw. She seemed a million miles away from him and he didn't know how to reach her. "Are you all right?"

"I'm fine. Dr. Harknis said everything is normal." She looked back down at her knees and smoothed the blanket. "It means so much to Daddy, seeing me win in New York. I won't hunt this season, of course, but I would like very much to ride in the National."

He was conscious of a flash of jealousy. The goddamn horses. That was all that mattered to her. And the horse doctor too, one musn't forget that. "If the doctor agrees, who am I to quibble?" His voice sounded hard.

Cecelia looked at him appraisingly. He looked tense and tired. Why did she have to care so much, she thought painfully. Why couldn't she be as indifferent to him as he obviously was to her? "Come to bed," she said. And when he was lying there next to her and reached over to put a hand on her breast, she turned and generously gave to him the one thing that she thought he wanted from her.

Chapter Twelve

Cecelia had occasional bouts of morning sickness and she felt more tired than usual, but otherwise she was well. She told her father she was pregnant, as she had to account for her failure to hunt, but for the time being she said nothing to Jenny. Her daily routine did not vary. The only apparent change in her life was that Gil seemed to be home a little more frequently.

He was sitting having breakfast with her one morning when Jenny appeared, a look of mingled apprehension and defiance on her pretty face. Cecelia, whose stomach was not dealing well with the plate of eggs in front of her, looked at her stepdaughter and said instantly, "Go upstairs and change. You are not going to school in those grungy jeans."

Jenny's voice was high-pitched and whining. "*Everybody* wears jeans, Cecelia. Why can't *I*?"

"I don't care what everybody else wears," Cecelia gave the age-old response of all mothers. "I am only interested in you. Change. Now."

"But I don't see why . . ." Jenny was beginning when Gil cut in.

"I don't want to hear another word out of you, Jennifer. Do as Cecelia says." It was the voice that always exacted instant obedience. Without another word Jenny left the room. Gil turned to his wife.

She was very pale and looked distressed. "Has Jennifer been giving you trouble?" he asked, real concern in his voice.

She essayed a shaky smile. She was going to be sick, she knew it. "Not really. She's just being a normal kid and testing the limits. It can be wearing but it has to be expected." She went even paler. "Excuse me," she mumbled and fled from the table.

Gil did not understand and thought she was upset about Jennifer. He thought for about the thousandth time recently that he had put a terrible burden on Cecelia's young shoulders when he had married her. It was never easy to cope with the problems of a preadolescent girl; it was less easy when you were only twenty-two years of age yourself. He would talk to Jennifer.

The result of his talk was a very subdued Jennifer. She was so subdued, in fact, that Cecelia became worried. She went into the child's room after school a few days later and sat on the bed. "Is something wrong, Jenny?" she asked. "You've been awfully quiet lately. Did something happen in school?"

"Nothing's wrong," Jennifer returned a little gruffly. She was very busy putting her books on her desk.

"Yes there is. I can tell. Can't I help? That's what I'm here for, you know."

"Daddy said I wasn't to bother you," Jennifer mumbled.

Cecelia felt a flash of annoyance. "Why not?" she asked. "And you don't bother me."

"He said," Jenny almost whispered to her desk, "he said you were having a baby and that I should leave you alone."

Now Cecelia was more than annoyed; she was angry. What was the matter with Gil? He wasn't usually this stupid. "Yes, I am having a baby," she said gently. "I was going to tell you myself. But that doesn't change how I feel about you. I love you. And you don't bother me."

Finally Jenny turned to look at her. "You'll be the baby's mother," she said.

Cecelia held out her hand. "Come and sit next to me." When she had Jennifer next to her on the bed she went on slowly, "I'm *your* mother too, aren't I?"

"I don't know," came the muffled response.

"Well, I am." She put an arm around Jenny. "Lots of kids have more than one mother. They have the mother who brought them into the world, of course, and then—if something happens so that she can't take care of them, or if she dies—they have a second mother. The second mother is their real mother too, you know, if she loves them and takes care of them the way I do you. There's no law that says a person has to have only one mother."

"I guess not," said Jenny thoughtfully. Then, "Do you love Daddy, Cecelia?"

Cecelia swallowed. "Yes, honey, I do. That's why I'm having a baby."

"Oh." There was silence as Jenny sat, thinking. Finally she said, "Do you think it'll be a girl?"

"We'll just have to wait and see."

Jenny smiled. "I could help you take care of it."

Cecelia grinned at her. "I certainly hope so. Babies always depend on their big sisters for help."

Jenny's eyes began to shine. "I'll be a big sister. Like Meredith is to Jason."

"That's right." Cecelia gave her a gentle push. "Come on now, get changed. Poppy is waiting to give you your lesson."

"Okay," said Jennifer. But instead of getting up she turned and hugged Cecelia. "I love you," she whispered.

When Gil arrived home that evening Cecelia was on the phone. He came into the bedroom and she looked up from her chair and smiled at him. "I can't believe it," she said into the telephone. "What did you do?" There was a pause and then she began to laugh. "I would love to have seen you," she said.

Gil went into the bathroom, and when he came out she was still talking. "It sounds like fun," she was saying regretfully, "but I don't think it would be Gil's thing at all. Why don't you and I get together for lunch one day?"

Gil walked slowly over to his closet and began to change his shirt. Cecelia hung up. "What was that all about?" he asked casually.

"That was Janet Osborne, a good friend of mine. She had a Fulbright to study in Europe and then she bummed around the Continent for a few months. It sounds like she had a ball." Cecelia's face was still bright with amusement.

"What was the invitation you refused so gracefully?" He looked very grave.

"Oh, it was just a party of kids from college. Beer and pizza, that sort of thing."

"Not my style, in fact," he said.

She grinned. "Not at all. It isn't mine either just now. I get nauseous at the very thought."

"Are you sure?"

"Absolutely." She leaned back in her chair. "How was your day?"

He was too old for her. It was the inevitable conclusion of all his tortuous thoughts. He should have left her to the boys of her own age, to Tim Curran, who was so obviously in love with her and who inhabited the kind of world in which she was comfortable. If he had had to marry again it should have been to someone like Liz, someone who was of his world and his generation. Someone who would have spent his money and hostessed his parties and sent his daughter off to boarding school without a second thought. He should not have married Cecelia; gallant, loving Cecelia, who, having been forced to marry him—he had gotten to that low point in his misery—was doing her level best to be a good wife to him and mother to Jennifer.

It hurt him unbearably to see her look at him warily, so obviously trying to assess his mood, to say and do the right thing. It hurt him and it made him angry; he was always shorter with her than he meant to be. He had even ceased to make love to her very often. He felt like an intruder in her life, and after that disastrous scene of a few months ago, he thought she was a little afraid of him. The kindest thing he could do for her, he thought with a kind of grim despair, was leave her alone.

They were sitting watching a TV special one Friday night when the phone began to ring. Frank and Nora had gone to the movies and Cecelia made as if to answer it. "Stay there," said Gil. "I'll get it."

It was his father-in-law. "I must talk to Cecelia," Ricardo said tersely and Gil called to her.

"Hi, Daddy," she said. "What's up?" There was a brief pause and Gil, watching, saw her begin to frown. "I'll get hold of him," she said, "don't worry." She hung up the phone.

"What's the matter?" asked Gil.

"Vic is colicking badly and Daddy can't find Tim." She frowned harder. "It's Friday night—he'll probably be at Mario's." She looked around frantically. "Where's the phone book?"

"In my desk." He went to get it and read the number out for her to dial.

"Is Dr. Curran there, please?" she asked. Then, "May I speak to him?" She tapped her foot impatiently while she waited. "Tim? Cecelia. Thank God I've found you. Vic is colicking and Daddy says it's bad. Can you go out to the farm?" Pause. "Okay. I'll see you there." She hung up the phone and turned to Gil. "I'm going over to Daddy's."

"Cecelia," he said patiently. "It's after ten o'clock

and it's raining. Your father is there and the vet is coming. There's no need for you to go as well."

"You don't understand," she said. She walked to the door. "Vic is *my* horse, my hunter. I've had him since I was fourteen. I've got to go." She left the room and Gil could hear her feet on the stairs.

He walked to the fireplace which they had blazing against the chill autumn evening. He was staring somberly into the flames when Cecelia came back into the room. She had changed her skirt for jeans, and against the weather she wore a slicker and rubber moccasins. "I'll come with you," he said.

"You can't." She came and kissed his cheek. "The Rosses are out and there's no one to stay with Jenny."

"I'd forgotten," he said slowly.

She gave him a quick smile. "Don't worry. I'll be with Daddy and Tim."

He walked to the door with her and waited until the lights of her car had disappeared down the driveway. When he went back to look at the rest of the television show he was very white about the mouth.

He was still downstairs at three in the morning when Tim Curran brought Cecelia home. They came in the back door and Gil walked slowly through the house to meet them. The bright kitchen lighting shone mercilessly on Tim Curran's face. He looked, Gil noted almost clinically, exhausted. "I'm so sorry, Cecelia," he was saying as Gil came into the room.

Cecelia was facing Tim, her back toward Gil. "I know," she said comfortingly. "You did all you could, Tim, and I'm grateful." She reached out for a minute and gave him a brief hug. He was rigid between her hands. "Go home and get some sleep," she said softly.

Over her head Tim's eyes met Gil's. "Yes, I will," he answered Cecelia. The two men did not speak, and in a minute Tim had turned and gone back out to the yard. Cecelia turned slowly, wearily, and for the first time she saw her husband. He was standing with his shoulders against the kitchen door, motionless. The harsh kitchen lighting clearly showed her his face, but she could read nothing on it.

Hers was more accessible. There were dark shadows under her eyes and grief and weariness in the set of her mouth. "He died," Cecelia said.

For perhaps the first time in his life, Gil put someone else's need above his own. He stepped away from the door and held out his arms.

Cecelia took two stumbling steps across the kitchen and then she was held close to him, his warmth and strength against her cold, shivering misery. She began to cry. He lifted her in his arms and carried her through the house and up the stairs to their bedroom. Her face was buried in his shoulder and he could feel the sobs racking her slender body. "I know, baby," was all he said, not trying to comfort her with words but only with his understanding.

He set her on her feet after he had closed the bedroom door behind them and stripped off her slicker. Her hands had been like ice as they clasped his neck. He steered her to a chair and said, "Sit down." His calm manner was taking effect and her sobs began to slow. She sat down and he went into the bathroom and turned on the tub. He came out, said, "Wait right there," and went out the door. When he came back he was carrying a glass of brandy which he handed to her. "Drink it," he said. She lifted a shaking hand and his own warm strong fingers closed over hers, guiding and steadying them. When the brandy was finished he went back into the bathroom and turned off the water. "Come on," he said to her. "Get into that hot tub and soak."

She had left her moccasins downstairs in the mud room, and he knelt in front of her now and took off her socks. "Stand up," he said and she did, allowing him to undress her and lead her into the bathroom.

The hot tub felt very good and her grief began to give way before weariness. She managed to get herself out and dried before Gil came in with her nightgown. He put her into bed, and when he got in himself next to her she said, her voice not quite steady, "Gil?" He turned and took her into his arms and she pressed her cheek against his shoulder, unspeakably comforted by his understanding, his undemanding care.

"Go to sleep, baby," he murmured, and relaxed and warm in the security of his arms, she did.

She awoke from habit three hours later in the first gray light of morning. She moved cautiously so as not to awaken Gil, sleeping so deeply next to her. His arm was still around her.

But he was evidently not sleeping as deeply as she had thought for he woke almost as soon as she stirred. "You're not getting up?" he mumbled.

"I have to." She pushed her loose hair behind her ears. She was still leaden with fatigue. "Jenny's class is going on a field trip today and I promised I'd go along to help Mrs. Arnold."

Gil looked very young with his sleep-tousled hair hanging over his forehead but his voice was full of authority. "You are not going anywhere today. You are staying in bed for at least the remainder of the morning. You look exhausted. Let someone else go."

"There isn't anyone else," said Cecelia. "I've already called. Everyone's either busy or working. And I cannot leave Mrs. Arnold alone to handle twenty kids. She has thirteen boys in that class!"

He looked resigned. "I thought you went on the last field trip as well. Why is it always you?"

Cecelia sighed. "I'm room mother. And I'm available." She made as if to push the covers aside.

"Stay right where you are," said Gil.

"But . . ." She looked in wide-eyed astonishment as he got out of bed himself. "*I'll* go," he said flatly.

She looked even more astonished. "*You?*"

"Me. As a matter of fact, I'll probably have more success than you in keeping the boys in line."

She lay back against her pillows. "You probably will."

He yawned and rubbed his head. "Where are the little brats going?"

"To the aquarium at Mystic."

"Great. On a school bus?"

"On a school bus." She pushed back the covers. "You don't have to do this, darling. I'll be fine."

He gave her a look and she hastily pulled the covers back. "Go back to sleep," he said. "We'll see you later."

Cecelia was comfortably curled up in the morning room with a book when her husband and stepdaughter returned in the afternoon. Jenny came into the room first and Cecelia put down her novel. "How was the trip?" she asked.

"Great." Jenny flopped on a sofa and kicked off her shoes. "Daddy took the whole class out for ice cream on the way home! It was super."

"I'll bet it was," said Cecelia. "I hope the ice cream was a reward for you all behaving yourselves."

"We were terrific," Jenny replied virtuously.

"Even Jason Murray?"

"Even Jason Murray. He started to make funny noises on the bus and Daddy told him to quit it. You know that voice of Daddy's—the *quiet* voice that's so much worse than anybody else's yelling."

"I know," said Cecelia.

"Jason shut up like a clam," reported Jennifer complacently. "And he stayed with the group the whole time we were there."

"You actually mean nobody got lost?" asked Cecelia incredulously.

"Nope. I mean yes. I mean nobody got lost." Jenny giggled. "Mrs. Arnold said she wished Daddy would come on *all* our field trips."

Cecelia grinned. "What did your father say?"

"He said he'd enjoyed himself. That's when he took us to Friendly's for ice cream. I wish," said

Jennifer, "he *would* come on all our field trips. He makes those dumb boys behave."

On this accolade Gil entered the room. "What do you mean 'dumb' boys?" he asked his daughter with mock severity. "I think I resent that."

"Oh, Daddy," she said with great world-weariness. "They *are* dumb. They make noises and say stupid things. Girls are much smarter."

Cecelia started to laugh and Gil said with amusement, "Talk to me about it again in a few years. I'll bet you'll change your mind." He looked at his wife. "How are you feeling?"

"Much better." She smiled at him.

"I forgot," said Jenny in a very small voice. "I forgot about Vic." Her eyes were full of tears.

"I know, honey. It's all right. Go on upstairs now and change your clothes." Cecelia's voice was very gentle.

The tears spilled over and Jenny dashed from the room. Gil stared after her in bewilderment. "How can anyone change so quickly? She was bright as a button a minute ago."

"Girls of Jenny's age are very changeable," Cecelia reassured him. "One has to be flexible. Now tell me, how did you survive your day?"

His face broke into the sudden boyish grin that was her favorite of all his smiles. "It wasn't bad at all," he said. He sat down in a comfortable armchair and stretched his legs in front of him. "They had a dolphin show. I'm a sucker for dolphin shows."

"Jenny was ecstatic." Cecelia chuckled. "She said you even got Jason Murray to behave."

"Um." He looked at her from under faintly

knitted brows. "You know, Mrs. Arnold is a very nice woman, but those kids walk all over her."

"I know." Cecelia sighed. "She's a very creative teacher and the girls love her. But she's not very good at disciplining the boys."

"You can't teach if the class is out of order."

"I know," Cecelia repeated. She arched a perfect brow at him. "I hear she invited you to come along on all future trips."

"Yes," came the astonishing reply. "I told her I'd try."

Cecelia could feel her eyes enlarging. "You did?"

He laughed a little harshly. "Don't look so shocked."

"I didn't mean to . . ."

"I know." He stared broodingly at the patterned rug at his feet. "You see," he offered, trying to explain a little, trying perhaps also to apologize, "I never had a family life, not the way you had. There was always a nurse to take care of me when I was small, and when I was old enough I went away to school." He gave her a fleeting look. "I don't mean I was neglected or anything. But I never learned the give-and-take of family life." He grinned. "My mother would no more have dreamed of going on a class field trip than she would have dreamed of shopping in a discount store."

"I see," she murmured very softly.

"I think Jenny was happy I came today," he said.

"She was, as I believe I mentioned earlier, ecstatic."

"I love my daughter," he said, his eyes still on the rug. "It may not always show, but I do."

"I know you do, Gil," replied Cecelia gravely. "I've always known that."

"Well. I'll drive with Frank over to your father's and bring back the wagon."

"Okay. It's in the stable yard."

He nodded absently and left the room. His wife did not pick up her book again but sat for quite some time staring blindly into space. It was true that she had always known he loved Jenny. It was because he loved Jenny that he had married her. He had wanted someone whom Jenny was fond of and who would be good to her. Lucky Jenny, thought Cecelia with great desolation, to have his love. She herself had to settle for kindness. And it was not enough.

Chapter Thirteen

❧

On Tuesday evening, November 3, Gil and Ricardo, both wearing black-tie evening dress, sat together in a reserved section just above the ring at Madison Square Garden in New York City. It was the opening night of the National Horse Show, a traditional society event, and all around Gil, dressed in black tie or gowned and jeweled, were a great number of familiar faces. Between him and his father-in-law sat Jennifer. Cecelia was somewhere down below them; she was to ride in the opening class of the opening night, a $2500 Open Jumper stake.

She had acquired another horse. Three weeks ago Maisie Winter called and asked her to ride a jumper of Maisie's called Fairhaven. Maisie's daughter-in-law had been riding him all summer and he had been doing fairly well in Open Jumper competition. "But, quite frankly, I think he can do better," said Maisie to Cecelia. "When Judy broke her ankle I'm afraid I wasn't as sorry as I should have been. Will you ride him for me, Cecelia?"

Cecelia had gone down to Maisie's, tried him,

and accepted. "He's a tremendously strong jumper," she told her older friend. "He'd do splendidly on the big European courses."

"I've had the feeling all year that he could do better than he has been. Perhaps I'm wrong. But I know that if he has the capacity, you'll find it," Maisie had returned confidently.

Ricardo was delighted that Cecelia had two horses to show. He explained to Gil as they sat waiting for the show to open that it was not the horse who was named show champion in the Open Jumper competition but the rider. Quite simply, the trophy for Leading Open Jumper Rider was awarded to the rider gaining the greatest number of points on one or two horses in the Open Jumper division. Points were awarded for all ribbons won. "Naturally," said Ricardo as he returned the wave of a person a few rows away, "a rider with two horses has a better chance of accumulating a large number of ribbons than a rider with one horse."

"Naturally," murmured Gil.

A very elegant-looking man in a military uniform came over to Ricardo. The two men spoke briefly and then Ricardo turned. "Colonel Carbone, may I introduce my son-in-law, Gilbert Archer." Gil shook hands, murmured a few pleasantries and then watched Ricardo as he went with the colonel to speak to the group of people sitting with him.

Jenny was looking intently through her program. She was dressed in a midnight-blue velvet jumper and satin blouse and looked, her father thought proudly, positively angelic. "Look, Poppy," she said to Ricardo as he returned and took his seat. "Here's your name." Both Gil and Ricardo looked and there, on the page devoted to the National Horse Shows Association officers was the name "Ricardo Vargas." "Wow," said Jenny and Gil and Ricardo smiled at each other over her head.

"Your father's name should be here as well, *niña*," said Ricardo. He flipped the pages until he came to the list of National Horse Show loge subscribers. "There." He pointed. "Mr. and Mrs. Gilbert Archer" looked back at them from the page and Jenny sighed.

"When I get bigger can I have my name in the catalog?" she asked.

"When you get bigger your name will be right here," said Ricardo, and he turned the page to the list of International Equestrian Teams. Represented this year were the United States, Canada, Great Britain, and Italy.

"Well, we'll see," said Gil temperately. He was not so sure he wanted to see his daughter devote her life to horses. It was a pleasant enough pastime, he supposed, but it could be taken to extremes.

There was a stir in the audience as the announcer came over the loudspeaker. The show was about to begin and it was opening with the Open Jumper stake in which Cecelia was riding both Czar and Fairhaven. The show had actually started in the morning and competitions had been held in the afternoon as well, but this was to be Cecelia's first class. Gil looked intently at his program at the note under the class listing. He read:

Time First Round. To be shown over eight or more jumps 4 to 6 feet in height with spreads from 5 to 7 feet. The first round is decided by adding together the faults incurred over the course and any penalties for exceeding Time Allowed to complete the course. The time taken to complete the course will decide between any horses with clean rounds or equal faults. Table II, Sec. 1. Touches not to count.

"What the devil does all this mean?" Gil asked Ricardo.

"Look! There's Cecelia!" cried Jenny. Gil looked up and saw a group of riders, dressed in black coats, tan breeches, and highly polished boots walking around the course. He recognized Cecelia instantly, even with her hair tucked up under a black velvet hat. She passed close below them but did not glance up. She looked very intent.

Ricardo turned to Gil. "It means that this class is conducted under the rules of the National Horse Shows Association, Table two, Section one of the rule book. They will jump only one round and they must do it within a specified time. If they go over that time they receive time faults. If they knock down a fence they receive four faults. If a horse refuses to take a fence it's three faults."

"Suppose more than one horse goes around without any faults at all?" asked Gil.

"Then the rider who had the fastest time wins," replied his father-in-law.

"I see," said Gil as the first rider came out of the gate, circled his horse, and cantered at the first fence.

"The problem spot on this course is going to be that big oxer and gate," murmured Ricardo.

The oxer he was referring to had a spread of seven feet; as the horse finished it he had to turn and take a vertical white gate that was five feet three inches high. Ricardo had hardly finished speaking when the horse presently on the course took off over the oxer. He made a fine jump, landed, turned, took two strides, and took off for the gate. He knocked it down. A murmur of disappointment came from the crowd.

Cecelia, riding Fairhaven, was the seventh rider out. No one before her had gone clean. Gil, Ricardo, and Jennifer all slid forward on their seats. Gil felt a tightening in his chest. The horse looked so big. The jumps looked so big. Cecelia looked so small. She circled the big gray gelding and took him smoothly over the first jump.

Fairhaven was a big, powerful horse, and Cecelia did not attempt to cut corners with him. As they approached the oxer Gil heard Jenny's breath hiss. He perfectly agreed. So far five out of the seven horses had come to grief on the combination oxer and gate.

Fairhaven took the oxer with ease. Cecelia turned him on a wide circle and let him take the gate head-on. He went over it smooth as butter and the audience broke into applause. Horse and rider took the rest of the course with the same seemingly unhurried ease and finished one second under the time limit, with no faults.

The next rider was Roderick Smith, a member of the USET and one of the leading riders in the world. He went clean and was four seconds under the time limit. By the time Cecelia came out on Czar, the next-to-the-last rider to take the field,

she was in third place with Fairhaven. Roderick
Smith was in first and Peter Anderson was in
second.

"Come on, Cecelia," muttered Jennifer. "You
can do it."

"She will be able to make better time on Czar,"
said Ricardo. "He is not so strong a jumper as the
gray, perhaps, but he is more athletic."

"Cecelia Archer," the announcer boomed, "riding
Czar Alexander." Cecelia circled and took Czar to
the first fence.

It was a very different ride from her ride on
Fairhaven. This time it was obvious from the start
that Cecelia was going for speed. She cut corners.
She brought Czar into the big oxer with so small a
margin for takeoff that Gil was sure she would
crash. The chestnut cleared the spread, however,
and when he landed Cecelia turned him and took
the gate *on an angle*. This time it was Gil's breath
that hissed in his throat. Before his horrified eyes,
Czar cleared the gate, landing in perfect position
for the next jump. The angle had saved Cecelia
several seconds. Gil watched, almost forgetting to
breathe, as the horse took the last two jumps.
Cecelia finished eight seconds under the limit and
the huge, packed Garden burst into a storm of
applause.

The last rider was Roderick Smith. He was forced
to go for speed, and under the pressure of it, his
horse refused the gate after clearing the oxer.
Roderick brought him around and got him to take
it on the second try but by then he was over the
time limit. Cecelia took a first and a fourth and
Ricardo was jubilant.

"You see, *niña*," he said to Jenny as the applause rolled out for Cecelia holding her trophy, "you see how all that hard work has paid off. All those long hours of training Czar to jump at angles were very necessary. The speed classes are not won on jumping big. They are won on the angles."

The applause died down as Cecelia and Czar left the ring. "Damn fine ride," said a man behind them. Jenny turned. "That was my mother," she announced proudly. Once again Gil and Ricardo's eyes met in a shared smile.

Cecelia joined them just before the intermission, still dressed in her riding clothes. She looked slim as a reed, although she had had to order new breeches for the show. Her old custom-made ones no longer buttoned.

"Where's your trophy?" demanded Jenny.

"I gave it to Frank to put in the car. He's waiting for you, Jenny. At the intermission it's time for you to go home."

"Oh, all right." Jenny's shoulders drooped but she didn't argue. They had had all this out before. When the five-gaited class was finished she allowed Gil and Cecelia to take her outside to Frank, who was waiting with the car.

"Be a good girl for Nora," Cecelia murmured, "and I'll see you Saturday."

"Okay," said Jenny docilely. Cecelia and Gil were spending the remainder of the week in New York while Jenny was going home to Connecticut. "You were super," she said. "I hope you win *all* your classes."

Cecelia laughed. "It's unlikely, but it would be nice. Good-bye, Jenny."

"Good-bye, sweetheart." Gil bent far down to kiss his daughter and for a minute she reached up to hug him. Then she was in the car and Frank was pulling away from the curb. Cecelia and Gil turned to walk together back inside. "I think your father knows half the audience," Gil said as they went up the escalator.

Cecelia laughed. "He does, I'm sure. He has such a good time at these shows."

"Are you sure you want to go to this party afterward? I don't want you to knock yourself out."

"We don't have to stay long but I think we should put in an appearance." It was a party given by the NHSA president. "I hate to bore you with all this horse talk, Gil," Cecelia went on with quick sympathy. "You've been so good about it."

"I don't mind the horse talk," he replied evenly. "I do mind you overdoing things."

"I'm not. I won't. We'll only stay a short while, I promise."

"All right," he agreed and they moved down the aisle to join Ricardo.

Gil was back at the Garden the following night to see Cecelia take a second on Czar and a fifth on Fairhaven. He did not see the Thursday afternoon class in which she took another first on Czar and third on Fairhaven. He was there Thursday night, however, for the jumping of the William C. Cox Memorial Challenge Trophy. It was a puissance stake and very different from the classes Cecelia had competed in previously.

" 'Puissance,' that means power, doesn't it?" Gil

asked Ricardo as they sat together in the now familiar seats and Gil looked through his well-worn program.

"Yes. This is a class for the 'super' horses, the horses who can jump enormous fences. It calls for a great deal of strength, and many very fine horses simply don't have it. Each rider is allowed only one horse in this class, but even if she were allowed two Cecelia would not have entered Czar. This kind of class is not for him. Fairhaven, on the other hand, may do very well."

"The international riders are in this as well?"

"Yes. It is open to all the jumping competitors."

"So how does it work?" Gil asked as he watched the crew raise the jumps to what looked like a very unsafe level.

"The course consists originally of six jumps. Those horses who go around clean come back and jump again. The second time the jumps are fewer but higher and wider. Eventually, in a good competition, only a wall and a spread jump will remain."

"Time doesn't count?"

"Time doesn't count."

"What is the highest a horse has ever jumped?" asked Gil with a sinking feeling in the pit of his stomach.

"Indoors?" returned Ricardo. "Seven feet three inches."

"Oh my dear God," said Gil. Now he knew why Cecelia had been so evasive when he asked her about this evening's class.

The first horse came out of the in gate and the announcer's voice came over the loudspeaker identifying him. Gil settled down rather grimly to watch. Cecelia was the tenth to ride, and by then four horses had gone around clean. "Cecelia Archer on Fairhaven," the announcer's voice informed them. "Mrs. Archer is wearing the sash that denotes she is presently our leading Open Jumper Rider." Cecelia put Fairhaven at the first fence, and with calm deliberation, he went around clean.

The first jump-off saw ten horses come out and six go clean. The second jump-off saw three go clean, and Fairhaven was one of them. As the men came out to raise the fences for the third jump-off Gil turned to his father-in-law. "This is insane. I would never have let her do this if I'd known what it entailed. For God's sake, Ricardo, she's pregnant!"

"Cecelia knows what she is doing," his father-in-law returned imperturbably. He turned to direct a penetrating brown stare at Gil's face. "She doesn't try to keep you from your work, does she?"

"It's not the same thing," said Gil.

"Why not? This is Cecelia's moment and she deserves it. She is one of the best natural riders over jumps I have ever seen—and I do not say that just because she is my daughter. She has an instinct that can't be taught—a feel for the stride of the horse, the position and height of the fence." The in gate opened and the Italian horse Fabrizio came into the ring. "Now watch," commanded Ricardo, and both men fell silent as the rider from the Italian Equestrian Team pointed his horse at the six-foot-ten-inch wall. The big black seemed to soar over it effortlessly and then took the spread with equal ease. "He is very good," murmured Ricardo.

"Who?" said Gil. "Horse or rider?"

"Both," answered Ricardo. "Here is Cecelia."

Gil's knuckles were white with pressure from his grip on his program. He watched his wife canter toward the fence and groaned to Ricardo, "She's going too slow!"

"No," said his father-in-law. "Three or four driving strides are all she needs before takeoff. Fairhaven has good impulsion." Almost as soon as Ricardo had finished speaking Fairhaven began to drive at the wall. Cecelia was well forward in the saddle, and as the horse left the ground she remained perfectly still. Having brought him properly to the jump, she sat quietly and let him take it without hindrance. And take it he did, smoothly and with his knees tucked well up. "Beautiful," said Ricardo as horse and rider proceeded to take the spread with equal confidence.

The third rider, Roderick Smith of the USET, did not have the fortune of the first two. His horse knocked down the wall and was out of the competition with a third. The jury announced that there would be a fourth jump-off between Giorgio Luchiani of the Italian Equestrian Team and Cecelia Archer. The wall would be raised to seven feet two inches.

"Jesus Christ," said Gil. He felt sick.

Ricardo said nothing as he watched the crew raising the height of the wall. "What is the highest Cecelia has ever jumped before?" Gil demanded of his father-in-law.

"Before tonight do you mean?"

"Yes."

"Six and a half feet."

"Great," said Gil. "That's just great. Suppose the bloody horse crashes?"

"He won't fall, Gil. Calm yourself." But for all his reassuring words, Ricardo looked pale. He had not expected Fairhaven to be this good.

The Italian horse and rider came out of the gate. Giorgio Luchiani was a veteran of many European puissance classes and he did not make the mistake of rushing the wall. The black made what looked like a successful jump but at the very end his hind feet nicked the top of the wall and knocked it down. "He took off too soon," said Ricardo. "That is always the temptation on these big fences. I hope Cecelia has the sense to wait."

The crowd burst into loud applause as Cecelia and Fairhaven came into the ring. They wanted to see her make the jump. Cecelia's face looked calm as she put Fairhaven into a canter and circled him before heading at the wall. "Seven feet, *niña*," muttered Ricardo. "Seven feet should be your takeoff. No more."

Fairhaven was approaching the wall now. It looked impossibly high, impossibly dangerous. Cecelia leaned forward and the big gray started to drive. Gil closed his eyes.

A tremendous roar went up from the crowd. Gil opened his eyes and looked. Cecelia was still in the saddle and heading for the spread. The wall was intact. "She did it," he said numbly.

"She did it," answered Ricardo. "With no experience, purely on instinct, she did it. She is a marvel. Bravo, *niña!*" he called as Fairhaven cleared the spread. The crowd rose to its feet in thunderous approval, and Cecelia turned and looked up at her husband and her father. She grinned and Ricardo raised his hand in a victory sign. Gil mimed huge relief and collapse and she laughed. From that moment on, Cecelia Archer was the darling of the Madison Square Garden audience. For the two days that remained of the show, she could do no wrong.

Chapter Fourteen

❧

On Sunday evening the National Horse Show closed with the presentation of the Leading Open Jumper Rider Challenge Trophy. The winner was Cecelia Archer. Her husband, her father, and her step-daughter were in the audience to watch her receive it.

At the party they attended after the show Cecelia was besieged by well-wishers. Gil withdrew a little from the press of the crowd and watched her. She was wearing her riding clothes and in them her long-legged figure still looked almost boyishly slim. She had taken her hat off and tied her hair neatly at the nape of her neck with a black velvet ribbon. Gil drank champagne and watched the clear-cut shape of Cecelia's small head as she moved from group to group under the chandelier lights.

After about an hour she sought him out and found him talking to Colonel Carbone, the coach of the Italian team. Gil smiled when he saw her and asked, "Ready to go?"

"Yes." She gave a bewitchingly sleepy smile to

Colonel Carbone. "All the excitement has worn me out, I'm afraid," she apologized charmingly.

"You were magnificent, Mrs. Archer," the colonel responded gallantly. "Your father—he is bursting with pride."

"He should be. He taught me everything I know."

The colonel kissed her hand. He turned to Gil. "And you, Mr. Archer, you are a lucky man."

"Yes," returned Gil pleasantly. "I am. Good evening, Colonel Carbone."

"Good evening," said the colonel. He bowed and moved away from them, and Gil and Cecelia turned together and walked to the door. They were staying once again in the apartment; Frank was coming in tomorrow with the van for the horses. Ricardo had spent the week with them but tonight he remained at the party after they left; he was having a splendid time, Cecelia was pleased to note. As Jenny had gone back to Connecticut with Frank, there was no one in the apartment when Gil and Cecelia arrived back at about one-thirty. Gil took Cecelia's coat and hung it in the closet for her.

"Would you like something to drink?" he asked.

"I'd love some orange juice," she answered and they both went into the kitchen. Cecelia poured her juice while Gil fixed himself a scotch.

She went to sit down at the kitchen table and he said, "Why don't you get those boots off first? They look terribly uncomfortable. Where's your bootjack?"

"In the bedroom." He went to get it and then helped her off with the high black dress boots. "Ah." Cecelia wiggled her toes. "That feels great."

She drank some of her juice. "Maisie told me tonight she was going to loan Fairhaven to the USET. Isn't that marvelous? I'll bet he wins an Olympic gold for them."

"Yet he's not as good a horse as Czar."

"He's a different kind of horse from Czar," she explained. "I think he'll come into his own in Europe. Their courses are very big and that's what he likes." She frowned a little and finished her juice. "Actually, I was wondering if I ought to lend Czar to the USET. I won't be riding for a while."

"No," he said definitely. She looked at him, startled by his peremptory tone. "I don't want you to loan Czar to anyone," he explained. "He's your horse and you did splendidly on him. He won for you this year and there's no reason why he shouldn't win for you again. The baby is due in May—you'll be riding by the summer."

She looked very surprised. "You wouldn't mind if I rode again next year?" she asked.

"Of course not." He spoke abruptly.

"Oh." She looked at him doubtfully. She had always received the distinct impression that he rather resented her riding, that he thought it took her away from other, more important, things.

"I was very proud of you this week," he said.

Her face began to glow. "Were you, Gil? I'm so glad. It meant so much to me to have you there."

She had opened the collar of her blouse and it fell away from her lovely slim neck. He looked at the pearly hollow at the base of her throat. It made him want . . . "Go to bed," he said harshly.

"You must be exhausted. I'll see you in the morning."

"Aren't you coming in?"

"In a little while," he answered.

She gave him a troubled look but said, "All right." She came around to the side of the table where he sat with a half-full glass of scotch in front of him. He didn't look up at her, and after a moment's hesitation, she kissed his thick silvery hair. "Good night, Gil," she said.

"Good night, baby," he returned evenly. She went inside and he finished his scotch, then went to pour himself another. He took the glass into the living room, where he sat down heavily in a cushiony chair and stretched his legs out before him. He had left the kitchen lights on, and the dim glow from down the hall was the only light in the room. Gil sipped his scotch and stared into the darkness and thought.

He thought of what Ricardo had said to him Thursday night as they watched the puissance class together. Cecelia didn't try to keep him from his work, Ricardo had said, so he shouldn't try to keep her from hers.

Ricardo had been right. He had always looked upon Cecelia's riding as a pastime, essentially trivial, completely expendable. He had never once thought of the years and years of sheer bloody hard work that had gone into it. When she talked about Czar he had listened politely, not really interested, not really thinking it important. He had been annoyed that she wanted to ride even though she was pregnant. If it had been at all a reasonable stand for him to take, he would have forbidden her to enter the show.

For the first time in his life the full extent of his own selfishness was being brought home to Gil. He had married Cecelia because he saw in her something very beautiful and very rare and he had wanted her. He had not once asked himself what she might want. He had married her and then expected her to mold her life to his. It had never even occurred to him that he might change his style of life to accommodate hers.

"Would you like more children?" she had asked him and he had said, "Yes." Never had he asked her what her thoughts were on the subject. Never had it concerned him that having a baby would force her to retire from the one activity she loved best in the world.

He had always lived his life as if the world revolved around Gilbert Archer. It was a bitter realization. What he had wanted he had taken. And if it didn't conform to his demands, he had smashed it. As he had almost tried to smash Cecelia on the terrible night he had first seen her with Tim Curran. As he had smashed Barbara. For the first time he realized his own responsibility for his first wife's reckless and unhappy career. She had loved him. And he had not cared.

He knew now a little of what she must have felt. He loved Cecelia. And Cecelia did not love him. After the way he had treated her, how could she?

He was luckier than Barbara had been, however, for Cecelia was kind. Her spirit was as lovely as her face and she would never willingly do anything to hurt him. She might love Tim Curran but she would hold to her marriage. Cecelia was not one to welch on her promises.

Which left him—where? In an impossible situation, he thought bleakly. She was his wife and he possessed her in every way, except in the only way he had finally come to learn mattered. He wanted her love—without that nothing else really mattered a damn. And her love was the one thing he did not have.

There was only one thing left that he could decently do and that was to leave her alone. He must refrain from pushing himself, his life, his friends or his job on her. He must allow her the freedom to do as she pleased. Oddly enough, he had no fears that she would fly into the arms of Tim Curran—or of anyone else for that matter. He had learned many things since he married Cecelia. Before he met her he had not thought very highly of women. All that had changed, he thought wryly, changed utterly. The future looked bleak indeed. How the hell was he going to leave her alone when he felt about her as he did?

In the weeks following the National Horse Show Gil tried scrupulously to adhere to the standard of conduct he had prescribed for himself. The result was to convince Cecelia that he had lost whatever interest in her he once had. Until now she had always had the dubious comfort of knowing that if he didn't love her properly, at least he found her sexually arousing. Now he didn't even make love to her anymore. She supposed it was because she was having a baby. He was very solicitious of her welfare, getting angry when he saw her lifting a heavy package, performing a hundred small services for her that would have warmed her heart if she thought they were prompted by his love and tenderness, not his sense of duty.

She was adequate to be the mother of his children but in every other aspect of wifehood he evidently found her lacking. She was too young, too inexperienced, to be a part of his larger world. It was the only conclusion she could draw from the way he constantly left her out of things, constantly refrained from inviting his friends and colleagues home. He had always given a Christmas party for the staff of *News Report,* she learned. She asked him if he would like to have it at The Birches this year. "I think it would be a nice gesture to offer them the hospitality of your home," she said hesitantly.

He looked at her, his mouth a little grim. How like Cecelia, he thought. Her thought for others never ceased to astonish him. "No," he said. "It would be too much for you. I'll have it at one of the New York hotels."

She started to protest that she would love to have his party but the words died in her throat. He looked taut as a strung bow as he stood beside her chair. He had lost weight over the last weeks. He was too thin; she thought he looked like a man living on his nerves. She was afraid something was very wrong but she couldn't ask him. She was afraid he was regretting his marriage. She was afraid he was seeing Liz Lewis in the city. He pulled out her chair and she stood up from the dinner table. "All right," she said quietly. "If that is what you would prefer."

"It is," he said quite firmly.

Chapter Fifteen

At the beginning of December Cecelia and Gil received an invitation to a party at Maisie Winter's home in Greenwich. Cecelia showed it to her husband that evening and remarked, "It sounds like fun. Would you like to go?"

"Of course," he answered, "if you think you would enjoy it." They had taken to treating each other with a relentlessly courteous reserve that wore on both their spirits.

"I'll have to break down and buy a gown in the maternity shop," Cecelia said. So far she was still managing to squeeze into some of her own clothes but a gown, she knew, would defeat her.

"Why not buy a whole new wardrobe?" he returned. "I want you to be comfortable."

She was pleasantly surprised by the attractiveness of the clothes she found in maternity styles. The gown she bought was quite elegant, she thought. It was a burgundy velvet with long sleeves, a plunging neckline that she filled out much better than she would have a few months ago, and an empire-style skirt. As they were getting dressed to leave for Maisie's Gil presented her with an early Christmas present: a rope of pearls. They were beautiful and looked luminous against the scarcely less luminous tones of her own skin. Pregnancy was agreeing with her.

"Thank you, Gil," she breathed, her eyes glowing.

"You're welcome," he replied. He did not smile. "Are you ready?"

She stood up from her dressing table. "Yes."

In the hall they kissed Jenny good-bye, then went out to the car. Gil was driving tonight as they weren't going very far. Neither of them spoke until the lights of Maisie's house glittered before them. It seemed, Cecelia thought despairingly, that they had even run out of polite small talk.

The party was very large and Gil and Cecelia were soon separated. There were quite a few people Cecelia knew and ordinarily she would have enjoyed herself. But her spirit felt leaden. The weight of the pearls was heavy around her neck. How could she go on like this, she thought. If only she didn't care so much! She pretended to listen to the conversation of Ben Carruthers and looked, automatically, for Gil. At last she found him. He was standing in a deep window recess and talking very seriously to Liz Lewis. Cecelia's hand jerked and some of her ginger ale spilled. Ben was immediately all concern and she forced her attention back to him. "It's fine," she assured him as she brushed at her skirt. "It's only ginger ale. I haven't been drinking anything alcoholic because of the baby."

"Let me get you some more," said Ben, and smilingly she agreed.

"You don't look well," Liz was saying bluntly to Gil. "You don't look as if you've been getting enough sleep."

"I'm fine," said Gil curtly. Automatically his eyes searched the crowd for Cecelia. He found her talking to Ben Carruthers. Liz followed his eyes.

"Cecelia looks beautiful tonight," she remarked. "But then, she always looks beautiful."

"Yes," said Gil. A muscle flickered next to his mouth.

"Have you two had a fight?" asked Liz.

Gil laughed and the sound was not pleasant. "A fight?" he repeated. "With Cecelia?"

She looked at him steadily. She knew him very well. She loved him very much. "What's wrong, Gil?" she said quietly.

He sighed. "I'm too old for her, Liz, that's all." He sounded very tired.

"Do you think so?" Liz's own voice had a peculiar intonation.

"Yes." He smiled at her crookedly. "Would you care to dance?"

"Why not?" she answered and they moved toward the dance floor in the adjoining room.

Two hours later Cecelia slipped off upstairs to the bedroom Maisie had set aside for the ladies. She was beginning to get a headache and she wanted a few minutes of quiet. She opened the door and there, seated before the dressing table putting on fresh lipstick, was Liz Lewis.

"Oh," said Cecelia. Then, getting a grip on herself, she came into the room. "How are you, Liz?" she asked with creditable calm.

"Fine," replied Liz flatly. Then, "I don't think Gil looks very well, though."

Cecelia sat down on the chaise longue and briefly closed her eyes. "No," she said. "He's been working too hard."

"Hard work never tired him out before," remarked Liz. She turned around and looked at Cecelia. "But then, he's not as young as he used to be."

Cecelia looked astonished. "Gil?" she said.

Liz laughed. "I thought as much," she answered cryptically.

"I beg your pardon?" Cecelia felt stiff and she was also beginning to feel angry.

Liz picked up her evening purse and stood up. "I've know Gil for a long time," she told his wife, "and there is one area where he has always underestimated his power. He has a very good idea of his talents as a journalist, a businessman, a sportsman, but he doesn't understand his power over women."

Cecelia sat perfectly still, frozen. Liz continued, "Oh, he knows he's good. He's no fool. But what it means to us to lie in his arms . . . no, he doesn't understand that." Liz's mouth curved into a bitter smile. "He never meant to be cruel, you see, not to Barbara, not to me." There was a pause as she looked at Gil's wife. "He thinks he's too old for you," she said abruptly.

"What?" Cecelia stared at her.

Liz laughed and this time she sounded genuinely amused. "Yes. He told me so just now. Isn't it funny?" She walked to the door. "I don't like you, Cecelia," she said. "You really can't expect that I should."

She was gone and Cecelia sat down again, motionless, trying to take in what Liz had been saying to her. What did it mean? What *could* it mean? It was fifteen minutes before she left the shelter of the bedroom. She wanted to go home. She had something she had to say to Gil.

It proved more difficult than she had thought. Their ride home was not as silent as the ride to the party had been. Gil kept up a light stream of amusing comment the whole way and she found it impossible to get around his shield of small talk. It was only upstairs, in their bedroom, that he finally fell silent. She sat in front of her dressing table, took off her pearls, and said, "Will you unhook this dress for me, Gil?"

He came over and stood behind her. She felt his hands on her neck undoing the hooks and then he ran the zipper smoothly down for her. The dress slipped off her shoulders and she slid her arms free of the sleeves. He hadn't moved away from behind her and his hands came down, very briefly, to touch her bare shoulders. Cecelia leaned back against him and reached to pull his hands down to cover her breasts. She felt rather than heard the sudden shocked intake of his breath. He tried to pull away from her, but she kept her hands over his, forcing them to stay where she had placed them. After a minute he jerked angrily out of her hold and went over to stare out the window. He was still in his evening shirt and black tuxedo trousers. "What was that all about?" he asked over his shoulder. He sounded a little breathless, as though he'd been running.

She didn't answer immediately but swung around and regarded his back with troubled eyes. Why was he behaving like this? If she simply did not interest him, he would not have had to tear away from her and put half the room between them. He might behave that way if he found her repulsive of course. But she did not think he found her repulsive.

"Gil," she said. Her throat was aching and tears began to glimmer in her eyes. "Darling, please look at me."

He turned around, reluctance in his whole bearing. He was white around the nostrils. "What do you want?"

She was frightened by the way he looked. Suppose she was wrong. Suppose he *did* find her repulsive. The months of strain took their toll and the tears spilled over and a sob broke from her aching throat. Through the blurring in front of her eyes she saw him take a step toward her. "Cecelia," he said. "What is the matter?"

She tried to stop the sobs but could not. He was bending over her chair now. "Baby, please stop crying. What's wrong?" She reached her arms up around his neck and clung to him, her face buried in his shoulder. He lifted her out of her chair.

"I love you so much," she sobbed into the crisp white pleats of his dress shirt. "And you don't love m-me."

"Not love you?" His arms were hard around her and she clung even tighter. "What do you mean, I don't love you?"

"You don't." She hiccuped. "You only married me because of Jenny. And it's br-breaking my heart."

"Cecelia," he said and his own voice was unsteady now. "My love, my darling, my angel. I don't know what you are talking about."

She raised her tear-streaked face to his. "You married me because you wanted a mother for Jenny."

He stared down into her wet face, his own face looking very strange. "Is that what you think?"

"Yes."

"Well, it's not true." He smoothed her hair away from her flushed cheek. "I married you because I loved you." He seemed to collect himself and then he said, very carefully, "Why did you marry me?"

"Because I thought you were the most wonderful man in the world and because I loved you."

"And what," he continued steadily, "of Tim Curran?"

Her eyes widened. "What has Tim got to do with it?"

"I thought perhaps you might love him."

Her large brown eyes looked into his own. For the first time in months he made no attempt to veil his expression. She pulled back from him. "Gilbert Archer," she said breathlessly, "I can't believe you could possibly be that stupid."

"Where you are concerned I can be very stupid indeed." His hands had dropped from her shoulders when she stepped away. "Tell me, Cecelia," he said softly, "tell me how stupid I've been."

Her dress had slipped to the floor when she had stood up and now it lay around her feet in a pool of rich, dark velvet. She wore only a strapless bra and a lacy half-slip. Her hair had started to tumble from its elegant knot and fell in silky strands across her shoulders. "I love *you*," she said to him. "I always have. I always will."

His face had altered radically at her words. "These last months I've thought I would give my very soul to hear you say that," he said slowly, deliberately, after a long pause. "I've thought I would go mad with longing for you. But I could never forget the circumstances under which you married me."

"What circumstances?" she asked.

"I practically blackmailed you, Cecelia, you know that." The white pinched look had come back about his nostrils.

"You paid Daddy's hospital bills, is that what you mean?"

"Yes," he said.

She looked up at him and felt weak with love. The poor darling—all this time he had been thinking . . . "I didn't need to be blackmailed," she said. "Is that really why you thought I married you?"

"Yes," he said again. He managed a crooked smile. "It's been a very salutary experience, let me tell you. For the first time in my life I realized that my own desires were not necessarily the law of the earth."

She touched his cheek. "I would like it very much," she said softly, "if you would kiss me."

He bent his head and his lips on hers were very gentle. She put her arms around him and under her hands the muscles of his back felt taut with tension. "Gil," she breathed as his lips left hers to move caressingly across her cheek, "darling, I won't break."

"I'm afraid you will," he said a little bleakly. "I'm afraid this whole scene is just the product of your unbelievably kind heart."

"Don't be an ass," she snapped, not at all kindly, and pushed him away. "Or at least don't be more of an ass than you've already been." She put her hands on her hips and glared at him. "What kind of a simp do you think I am? If I loved Tim Curran I would have married him. This isn't the Dark Ages anymore. Girls don't get married because the landlord threatens them with eviction, for God's sake. I married you because I loved you. Although if I'd known what a colossal idiot you could be . . ."

"All right! All right!" For the first time since they had come upstairs the muscles in his face had relaxed. Then he began to laugh. "I'm sorry. You're right—as usual."

"Well then," she said severely, "kiss me properly please."

He obliged her instantly. Crushed against him, feeling the hardness of his strong lean body pressed against hers, she gave herself up completely to the kiss. He felt the abandonment in her mouth. "Christ," he said. "Cecelia." He kissed her throat, her shoulders, her mouth again. Still locked together, he began to move her toward the bed.

It didn't take very long to rid themselves of the remainder of their clothing. Then they were down on the bed together. There was hunger in Gil's caresses—she could feel it—but there was also a care that melted her heart even as his passion

enflamed her body. Her breasts swelled with longing under his fingers and he moved his lips gently
across the soft swell of her belly under which beat
a new life.

She slid her fingers into his thick silky hair.
"Gil," she whispered. His hand moved slowly down
over her hip to her thigh and began to move
caressingly. She whimpered and her body arched
involuntarily toward him. She reached to draw
him closer, open and aching for him to come and
create the fulfillment they both needed.

He had wanted it to be a prolonged lovemaking.
He had wanted to go slowly and with care, to give
her every pleasure he possibly could. But when
she tugged at him and cried his name like that, it
was no longer possible to delay. It was no longer
possible to be gentle and careful. Nor, it seemed,
did she want him to be.

It was an intense and passionate lovemaking in
which they gave each other a great deal more than
physical pleasure. When they finally lay quietly,
wrapped in each others arms, they felt the profound contentment that only comes when love is
present.

After a while she stirred and softly kissed the
strong column of his throat. "I adore you," she
whispered huskily.

He put his cheek against her hair and held her
closer. "I wish I were the emperor of the world,"
he said after a while, "because then I could lay it
at your feet."

She thought for a minute. "I'd like that."

He chuckled. "Of course you would. Think of
the horses."

"Since I can't have the world, however," she went on serenely, her cheek still pressed against his shoulder, "I'll settle for you."

He stroked her hair with gentle fingers. "I've done a lot of thinking over these past months, Cecelia, and I promise you things will be different. I can't promise you a nine-to-five job, because *News Report* will never be that, but I can be home a lot more frequently than I have been."

She moved away from him a little so she could see his face. "Do you mean that?"

"Yes." He spoke quietly, gravely. "I can see now what an abominably self-centered person I've been—first with Jenny and then with you. It simply never occurred to me that when I acquired a wife and a child I would have to make some adjustments in my own life-style. I never thought about it at all—that's the worst part." He looked at her and his gray eyes were darker than usual. "When it finally dawned on me that I scarcely ever saw you—and I missed you like hell on that European trip—it also occurred to me that maybe you liked it that way. You seemed so busy, so satisfied, with your father, the horses, Jenny."

"I was busy," she replied. "But not satisfied."

He smiled a little although his eyes remained grave. "What brought on this—confrontation—tonight? Why did you suddenly bring all this out into the open?"

She hesitated and then told him part of the truth. "It was something Liz Lewis said to me tonight. It made me start to think. I had thought, you see, that you had simply lost all interest in me.

Liz's comment made me think that perhaps there was another explanation."

"What did Liz say?"

"She said you thought you were too old for me." Her large, expressive eyes held his. "I thought that if that were true, then perhaps there was a very different explanation for your odd behavior. I thought it was worth a try to find out."

"I see."

"You hadn't been near me in weeks," she went on steadily. "When I put your hands on my breasts tonight you pulled away like a scalded cat. Indifference wouldn't account for that."

"No. It wouldn't."

"So I thought—I hoped—that maybe you did love me after all and were staying away from me because you thought I didn't love you. It seemed incredible that you could be that dumb, considering the way I turned into jelly every time you looked at me, but then, I thought, maybe you *were* that dumb."

His eyes were smiling at her now. "I take it back," he said. "I'm not too old for you. *You're* too old for me."

She grinned. "Just stick with me, little boy, and you'll learn. The love of a good woman is all you need."

He looked interested. "Is that true?"

"Absolutely."

He moved toward her purposefully. "Then I suggest we begin the therapy," he said.

"Wait a minute," she protested as he took hold of her. "That wasn't what I meant."

"Don't argue," he ordered and kissed her quite thoroughly.

When he finally raised his head she gently traced a line around his mouth. Then she smiled at him, a smile of infinite sweetness, infinite seduction. "Argue?" she said softly. "I wouldn't dream of it."

TELL US YOUR OPINIONS AND RECEIVE A FREE COPY OF THE RAPTURE NEWSLETTER.

Thank you for filling out our questionnaire. Your response to the following questions will help us to bring you more and better books. In appreciation of your help we will send you a free copy of the Rapture Newsletter.

1. Book Title:_____

   Book #:_____ (5-7)

2. Using the scale below how would you rate this book on the following features? Please write in one rating from 0-10 for each feature in the spaces provided. Ignore bracketed numbers.

(Poor) 0 1 2 3 4 5 6 7 8 9 10 (Excellent)
                                        0-10 Rating

Overall Opinion of Book. . . . . _____ (8)
Plot/Story. . . . . _____ (9)
Setting/Location. _____ (10)
Writing Style. . . . . _____ (11)
Dialogue. . . . . _____ (12)
Love Scenes. . . . . _____ (13)
Character Development:
Heroine:. . . . . _____ (14)
Hero:. . . . . _____ (15)
Romantic Scene on Front Cover. . . . . _____ (16)
Back Cover Story Outline . . . . _____ (17)
First Page Excerpts. . . . . _____ (18)

3. What is your: Education: Age:_____(20-22)

     High School ( )1   4 Yrs. College ( )3
     2 Yrs. College ( )2   Post Grad   ( )4 (23)

4. Print Name:_____

   Address:_____

   City:_____State:_____Zip:_____

   Phone # (   )_____(25)

Thank you for your time and effort. Please send to New American Library, Rapture Romance Research Department, 1633 Broadway, New York, NY 10019.

RAPTURE ROMANCE

*Provocative and sensual,
passionate and tender—
the magic and mystery of love
in all its many guises*

Coming next month

MIDNIGHT EYES by Deborah Benét. Noble was as wary of Egyptian men as Talat was of American career women. Could their passion burn through the cultures that bound them?

DANCE OF DESIRE by Elizabeth Allison. Jeffery Northrop offered dancer Patrice Edwards love beyond her wildest dreams—but could she give up her hard-won independence in exchange?

PAINTED SECRETS by Ellie Winslow. He'd left her four years ago, but now Lawrence Stebbing was back. For Nadine's love—or their son?

STRANGERS WHO LOVE by Sharon Wagner. Was Paul Roarke really an easily bought-off fortune-hunter? Arianna didn't think so, until her new husband suddenly disappeared . . .

RAPTURE ROMANCE

Provocative and sensual, passionate and tender— the magic and mystery of love in all its many guises

(0451)

#13 ☐ SWEET PASSION'S SONG by Deborah Benét.
(122968—$1.95)*

#14 ☐ LOVE HAS NO PRIDE by Charlotte Wisely.
(122976—$1.95)*

#15 ☐ TREASURE OF LOVE by Laurel Chandler.
(123794—$1.95)*

#16 ☐ GOSSAMER MAGIC by Lisa St. John. (123808—$1.95)*

#17 ☐ REMEMBER MY LOVE by Jennifer Dale.
(123816—$1.95)*

#18 ☐ SILKEN WEBS by Leslie Morgan. (123824—$1.95)*

#19 ☐ CHANGE OF HEART by Joan Wolf. (124421—$1.95)*

#20 ☐ EMERALD DREAMS by Diana Morgan. (124448—$1.95)*

#21 ☐ MOONSLIDE by Estelle Edwards. (124456—$1.95)*

#22 ☐ THE GOLDEN MAIDEN by Francine Shore.
(124464—$1.95)*

*Prices $2.25 in Canada

Buy them at your local bookstore or use this convenient coupon for ordering

THE NEW AMERICAN LIBRARY, INC.,
P.O. Box 999, Bergenfield, New Jersey 07621

Please send me the books I have checked above. I am enclosing $_____
(please add $1.00 to this order to cover postage and handling). Send check
or money order—no cash or C.O.D.'s. Prices and numbers are subject to change
without notice.

Name_____

Address_____

City _____ State _____ Zip Code _____

Allow 4-6 weeks for delivery.
This offer is subject to withdrawal without notice.

SPECIAL $1.00 REBATE OFFER
WHEN YOU BUY
FOUR RAPTURE ROMANCES

See complete details on reverse

. Book Title _____

Book Number 451-_____

U.P.C. Number 7116200195-_____

. Book Title _____

Book Number 451-_____

U.P.C. Number 7116200195-_____

. Book Title _____

Book Number 451-_____

U.P.C. Number 7116200195-_____

. Book Title _____

Book Number 451-_____

U.P.C. Number 7116200195-_____

U.P.C. Number

0

SAMPLE

7 1162 00195

REBATE COUPON

SPECIAL $1.00 REBATE OFFER WHEN YOU BUY FOUR RAPTURE ROMANCES

To receive your cash refund, send:

1. This coupon: To qualify for the $1.00 refund, this coupon, completed with your name and address, must be used. (Certificate may not be reproduced)

2. Proof of purchase: Print, on the reverse side of this coupon, the *title* of the books, the *numbers* of the books (on the upper right hand of the front cover preceding the price), and the U.P.C. numbers (on the back covers) on your next four purchases.

3. Cash register receipts, with prices circled to:
   Rapture Romance $1.00 Refund Offer
   P.O. Box NB037
   El Paso, Texas 79977

Offer good only in the U.S. and Canada. Limit one refund/response per household for any group of four Rapture Romance titles. Void where prohibited, taxed or restricted. Allow 6–8 weeks for delivery. Offer expires March 31, 1984.

NAME_____

ADDRESS_____

CITY_____STATE_____ZIP_____